SURVIVOR

ALONE

JAMES PHELAN

KENSINGTON PUBLISHING CORP.

www.kensingtonbooks.com

KTEEN BOOKS are published by

Kensington Publishing Corp.
119 West 40th Street
New York, NY 10018

Previously published in Australia by Lothian Children's Books/ Hachette and in the United Kingdom by Atom Books.

All Kensington titles, imprints, and distributed lines are available at special quantity discounts for bulk purchases for sales promotions, premiums, fund-raising, educational, or institutional use.

Special book excerpts or customized printings can also be created to fit specific needs. For details, write or phone the office of the Kensington special sales manager: Kensington Publishing Corp., 119 West 40th Street, New York, NY 10018, attn: Special Sales Department; phone 1-800-221-2647.

KENSINGTON and the KTeen logo are Reg. U.S. Pat. & TM Off.

ISBN-13: 978-0-7582-8068-8
ISBN-10: 0-7582-8068-8

First KTeen Trade Paperback Printing: May 2013

10 9 8 7 6 5 4 3 2 1

Printed in the United States of America

For Tony and Natalie

From childhood's hour I have not been
As others were; I have not seen
As others saw; I could not bring
My passions from a common spring.
From the same source I have not taken
My sorrow; I could not awaken
My heart to joy at the same tone;
And all I loved, I loved alone.

—from "Alone" by Edgar Allan Poe

then . . .

My name is Felicity, she said. *I am recording this from my family home . . .*

She looked like she was about eighteen or nineteen. Blond hair, pretty face, kind of how I'd expected an attractive American girl to look. But these were the words this girl spoke into her camera every day: *Death. Screaming. Silence. Gunfire.* How our world had so quickly changed.

I'd found the camera on top of the TV and had been sitting on her couch, watching the footage for the past half-hour. Scattered around the living room were photos of a happy-looking middle-aged couple and the girl, Felicity.

"How many of you are left?" I asked aloud. Maybe she was now part of an endangered species. Maybe that's why she was keeping some kind of video diary, so she wouldn't be lost forever like everyone else.

I remembered the vacant forms of Dave and Anna and Mini as they lay there together: lost, silent, still.

My broken friends.

Back at 30 Rock, I'd ruffled their beds and served them food and pretended not to notice when I scraped it away, like I pretended not to notice so much else. I sat there on the observation decks and took it in shifts by myself. I was the one who broke through the locked door in 59C and used the typewriter in the study. I was the one who had shot a man dead in the street and watched him fall like a tree. My friends had been with me the whole time, but only I had seen them after that first day.

I'd met no other survivors since. I thought it was just me and the Chasers and the hint of those I'd seen from afar. But Felicity was *real*. Part of me burned to find her, to know that she was okay, a signal fire in my chest.

"Where are you now?" My voice was a whisper, as useful as a single clap in a crowd of applause. My breath fogged but it felt warm in here.

I fast-forwarded to her latest entry:

Earlier this morning I went out to look around for others like me . . . There seem to be groups of people out there but I'd only ever heard them at night. I was too scared to go out and approach them in case they shot me, or worse . . .

"But have you seen them?" I asked the screen. "Have you seen what they do?"

I remembered the first time I saw the Chasers. Among the group of people drinking rain and slush was another, smaller group, hunched over the dead bodies in the street. Like animals. In horror, I realized that their mouths were closed over the bare flesh of those bodies. They were *drinking* from them. They were drinking everything. Anything.

Felicity continued speaking. *Crazed people. They dip their mouths into pools of water as easy as they drink from the dying, from the dead.*

"You've seen them!" I wanted to punch the air in recognition. Felicity had seen them too. "You must be real. You must be okay."

Now I knew there really was hope, there really was a world out there, one with survivors like me. I could again let myself wonder what my friends were doing back home in Australia; school would be starting any day, our final year at high school. They'd have so many stories to tell of summer holidays. I'd give it all and then some to hear my dad's voice, to hear him tell me everything was okay there and that help was on its way—that it would be all right and that they all missed me, that I'd be home soon.

Even the thought of seeing my dragon of a step-mother seemed bearable. And maybe it was time to track down my real mum, if I could just . . .

Felicity turned her head to the side and listened to something off-screen. From the background, I could tell that she'd filmed herself with the camera perched on the coffee table. She was sitting on the leather couch I was sitting on now. She remained quiet, facing left, and I looked in that direction too—towards the door of the apartment. There was a banging noise coming through the camera's little speaker and it startled me and I saw that she'd also jumped at the sound.

She slid down from the couch and sat on the floor, close to the camera, but kept her face pointed towards the front door. I glanced at it again; I'd dead bolted it the previous night as soon as I'd come in.

I paused the video and listened. There it was again; a noise outside. I went to the window and peered through the curtains. No movement out there in the breaking dawn. Silence. A dead streetscape. That hadn't changed. My breath fogged against the glass as I waited, wrapped in a quilt, watching, searching, imagining.

I pressed play on the camera, just to hear her voice, worried that she would disappear as unexpectedly as she had arrived.

It's been twelve days since the incident . . .

I paused the tape again. Twelve days? Is that how long I'd been checking the phones and televisions and radios, wanting to hear the sound of anyone's voice other than my own?

Twelve days ago, I'd taken that subway ride from the UN Secretariat Building towards Lower Manhattan, a trip that saved my life and changed my world.

"I'd been on a leadership camp for senior students," I told her. "It was meant to teach us about how the world really worked. Some education."

I waited for her response. Of course it didn't come. But she was still more alive than the friends I'd had to let go. She was still real to me, so I continued talking to the screen.

"There was a bang and our train carriage rolled and it had been hot and then black and an hour or so later

I had come to and by dim flashlight I'd found my way to street level to find the power out and the phones dead. And that was the best of it."

I remembered seeing that unexploded missile in the street on the first day. All those craters around town, the buildings that had been reduced to rubble. It seemed too big an attack for terrorists. Far too big. Citywide, at least. What with all the radio and TV stations being out, the total lack of response from authorities. This had to be nationwide . . .

The little camera's battery light was flashing red, reminding me that I could lose Felicity at any moment. I had to be sure what she had said.

Was today day twelve? Or was that yesterday? Was she counting from the day after? Was it twelve nights that had passed? I started to feel uneasy about how carelessly I'd been marking time.

I pressed play again. There was silence on the camera too. I watched Felicity and she stared back at me. She spoke softer, quieter, closer to the camera:

At first I didn't see anyone. I stayed clear of Central Park because I've seen those sick people congregate there, thousands of them. But this morning I was out getting food, and I found a bicycle and started riding back. The sun was out and for a moment I forgot where I was, what was around me, how the world has changed . . . I ended up riding into the park, as I've done with my parents hundreds of times as a kid . . .

She shifted position, sitting up a little straighter and redirecting the camera's lens so that it didn't crop off the top half of her face.

It was the lower west corner; you can't see it clearly from here for the trees. I rode by a group of them. They looked sick, like the others I've seen. There were maybe fifty or more. But they were standing around a fire. And there was something about them—they seemed almost . . . friendly.

She looked down at her lap. Perhaps she was flexing and cracking her knuckles with anxiety like I was doing now.

It's about three o'clock. I'm going back to the park while there's still daylight. I'm going to see if I can talk to them, to that group.

She was still and watched the camera lens and I felt as though she was staring right at me. She wiped away a tear. *I'm sick of being alone.* She took a deep breath and let it out, her bottom lip quivering.

I had to meet her! A survivor, like me, someone unafraid to get out there on the streets and try to make something better.

I've been alone so long, lost so much, I don't know who I am anymore . . .

She reached forward and turned off the camera and before me the tiny screen went blue. I switched it off, the screen went black. It was time to go.

I moved fast. I wrote a hope note, the kind of thing I'd seen stuck to buildings around town and flittering through the air and sodden on the ground. The kind of thing you'd do for a missing cat, only these were for people, for loved ones. I scrawled on a piece of paper a few lines describing who I was and explaining that I'd be outside 30 Rock's entrance at the ice rink at ten o'clock every morning, and to please come and meet me. I left it next to the camera on the table and considered adding my own message on film, but I felt like it might taint what she'd done. Besides, I've never really liked myself on camera—my voice comes across all squeaky and strange, not my own.

I took some clean stuff from Felicity's dad's wardrobe—socks and underwear, a T-shirt, a flannel shirt—and got dressed. I pulled my jeans on, they still felt a little cold and damp but they'd do, found a knit cap in Felicity's room, put on my trainers which had dried out overnight and laced them up tight. I rebandaged my grazed hands, put on a black puffer jacket and zipped it up to my neck. I'd come here with nothing but the clothes on my back and my stupid little flashlight and I would leave with the same but at least feeling fresher.

I stood at the locked apartment door and pressed my ear against it. Silence. I listened for about five minutes. When I was as sure as I could be there was no one beyond the door, I unlocked it and went outside, with something like hope burning a hole in my chest.

now . . .

1

Manhattan was in bad shape. It was impossible to take it all in; I'd look at a half-collapsed building and completely miss the flattened dwellings either side of it. Even now, twelve days later, every view was a new scene of destruction—fires sending curls of smoke into the freezing cold air, the charred remains of buildings and vehicles beyond repair. I'd always known New York would be chaos—too big to ever feel familiar—but this wasn't the kind of chaos I imagined.

Yesterday, I'd been able to accept that my friends were dead because I'd realized they lived on through me. Anna, Dave, Mini—nobody could pry them away from me, but I accepted the meaning of being alone. I had promised myself that as the days became clearer and longer, that I would notice how the sun shone again. And as it did, so I would, because now, through Felicity, there was hope.

Since the attack, I'd been happy to stay as far above the destruction and chaos as possible. I'd spent almost every night high up in the building at 30 Rockefeller Plaza, where the Top of the Rock observation deck gave me 360-degree views. I'd slept a safe distance above the city streets, glassing with binoculars the destruction below, day and night. But I'd done my time up there waiting for salvation—an airlift, an armada, a convoy that had yet to come. There was only so long I could avoid going into the arena.

Last night had been as dark as a night could be. While I had never relished being down at ground level, the prospect of climbing the seventy-odd flights of stairs back to that place I'd called home, that place where I'd left my own messages on a window, was the more frightening prospect. All that darkness to overcome, only to be marooned up there, disconnected from the reality that existed on the ground among the lifeless masses. No, I didn't need to go back there, not alone, perhaps not ever. I took shelter at 15 Central Park West, Felicity's home. And now there was Felicity, or at least the possibility of her, so I had to find her.

I looked for her footprints in the street, but knew it would be impossible to distinguish hers from a Chaser's. Even though so much had changed since yesterday, the Chasers remained as real now as they had ever been.

I would always dream about the way their eyes seemed to lock onto mine as they turned from the lifeless bodies on which they were feeding. I would dream about the blood dribbling down their chins and staining their lips dark red.

The ponds in Central Park were the obvious place for them to go for water. Today, Central Park West was cold, but quiet too. The rain overnight had cleared a lot of the snow, dust, and ash from the streets, but there were still puddles of slush here and there, motionless and gray. I walked south a block, where the rising sun was high enough and the trees low enough so that I was bathed in light. I stood still in the sunshine. It was cold, but this shaft of sun was bright and it felt peaceful just to stand there until the clouds shifted and stole my warmth.

At the bumper of a car I took a muesli bar from my pocket and ate, the sugar and sustenance sharpening my thoughts and bettering my mood. Sure, I had to get out of here. But I knew something else now—to do that, I needed more than just me, a journey like that would be too much alone. Evade the Chasers alone, survive these savage streets—yes, I'd proved I could do that alone. But to get out of here, to get off this island city . . .

A deep, rumbling noise roused me from my thoughts.

I ducked down behind the car and listened. It sounded like a vehicle coming down the road from the north.

I crept forward and hunkered down against a taxi, careful to keep myself hidden. It was the noise of a big diesel engine, growing louder by the second. Soon it was so deafening that I knew it was definitely not a car like the one I'd driven around the city. A truck, maybe even a tank.

I crawled to the front end of the taxi, making sure I didn't bump it and give myself away. Still on my hands and knees, I held my breath so that it wouldn't show in the freezing air as I peeked around the front bumper.

A group of people.

Chasers? No, not this time.

About two hundred yards up the street, the men were purposeful, careful, and headed my way. Two big trucks inched along behind them, noisily nudging cars out of the way. As the procession neared, more details revealed themselves. They were armed and wore camouflage and black, from their boots to their helmets. From here they looked young. Boys into men, men into soldiers, soldiers into war. As if warfare had always been their destiny. Did we create wars or were they inevitable, the ultimate trading tool when everything else became too hard?

But there was no time to think about that now. The soldiers were coming.

2

utomatic gunfire rang out. Bullets pinged and zapped off metal and concrete. The soldiers were shooting. Falling glass and dust sent me sprawling. They were shooting at me.

I stayed behind the taxi and knelt closer to the side-walk in a tight huddle, my hands over my ears. I got as close to the ground as I could. I shook. My knees and forehead on the cold wet ground. My breath fog-ging before my face. I tried to move lower, to crawl my way into the earth.

The shooting stopped.

I took my hands off my ears, but I could still hardly hear. I closed my eyes. I'd already seen enough death and if it was coming for me now, I did not want to know in advance. Sound began to return, a ringing in my ears soon replaced by the thrumming engines of the trucks passing close. I heard walking, the crunch-ing of snow.

Someone was coming, closing. I opened my eyes.

I was pushed over, flat to the ground.

I looked up and a man with a rifle was standing over

me. Not at all the boy I'd imagined from afar. He had a short ragged beard, like he'd last shaved without a mirror, with a thick moustache covering his top lip. A gas mask hung under his chin, loose as if ready to pull on at a moment's notice. He wore a bulletproof vest over a plastic camouflage jumpsuit, a white parka over his shoulders. Black boots. Big black boots.

His rifle had a timber stock and a black steel scope, like a hunting rifle. It was steady in his hands, and pointed directly at me. I looked beyond this appendage to the man, and I realized his issue with me: *He thinks I'm a Chaser. Or worse, the enemy.*

I said, "Don't kill me."

His expression didn't change. The man's eyes, framed behind glasses, told what could have been a lie: that he didn't have it in him to kill me. Or that was what I chose to see. Every second of hesitation gave me hope. Here was a man standing over me, a man with his own choices to make, his own unpredictable nature to contend with.

"Please. Don't. Don't do it." I tried a smile, a friendly gesture. "Look, see? I'm not *sick* . . ."

My throat gave out with "sick"; a croaking, hoarse, feeble cry, all I had after so many days of soliloquy.

I showed him my empty hands, how I was unarmed, on the ground, at his mercy. Yesterday, maybe I would not have been so willing to submit, but today, now, I wanted to live, to hear what he had to say, to learn what was out there, to somehow get home.

I pleaded softly, "I'm not the enemy . . ."

He reached down and I inched away, shuffling back

in the wet snow from both the threat of his grasp and his pointed rifle, but he took a long stride after me and dragged me to my feet. He held me up by my collar, at arm's length, shaking me to see how I'd react. I didn't fight him. His three colleagues stood beside the pair of all-terrain trucks with their monster-sized tires and stared.

This man who held me turned around and shouted: "He's not sick."

"So?" one of his colleagues replied as he climbed back into the truck. Visible through the open back flap of the canvas-topped truck was a container the size of a small car with USAMRIID stenciled on the side of it.

"They said they were all sick . . ." the soldier holding me said quietly to himself, dangling me in midair, his gaze locked on mine.

"Forget him!" The shout rattled around the empty street. "We gotta hustle."

"Shoot him!" yelled another. "Do the kid a favor." He slammed the cab door of the second truck and it motored off in the cleared wake of the first.

The last soldier remained, watching closely from the other side of the street, cradling his rifle. If this one here doesn't kill me, that one will, won't he? I swallowed hard. Should I run? Twist away and run? Zigzag my way around debris and hope they miss?

"Please . . ." I said to the one who held me. He had a name tag on his vest: STARKEY. "Please, Starkey, I'm not sick. You *can't* kill me."

"Kill him!" The order echoed across the street. Guns

entitled men to do anything. They were clearly Americans, so why shoot me? Out of anger for what's happened here? Out of fear? No, these were outsiders. They probably knew what was going on here, they had *information*. I was more afraid than he could ever be.

I pleaded with my eyes. I didn't want to die, and now, more than that, I wanted to *know*. I wanted to talk, to ask questions, to listen and learn.

He let me go. "How old are you?"

"Sixteen," I replied.

"We're moving!"

"I'll catch up!" Starkey yelled across to his buddy, who shook his head and remained standing there, rifle slung in his arms like a child. "Where were you when this attack happened?"

"Here." I was too frightened to lie.

"Here in this street?"

"No," I said. "A subway; I was in a subway."

He nodded. "How many like you?"

"Like me?"

"Not sick."

"I don't know."

"How many are you staying with?"

"Just me."

"What?"

"I'm alone," I replied.

I could see what he was thinking. That I was crazy. That I'd probably just crawled out of some blackened, deserted building, completely out of step with what was going on, a raving lunatic. No matter what stirrings of sympathy he may have felt, he couldn't get away from the fact that I might just be mad and so, in my own way, just as dangerous as the infected people. Maybe I would have thought that too.

I tried to explain. "There's this girl—Felicity. She might be in Central Park still. That's where I'm heading. There might be others. I just haven't seen anyone in person—"

"Well, kid, *I've* seen a lot. I've seen good people do things that don't make no sense," he said, not looking at me. "No sense. You understand?"

I nodded. He'd done stuff, too, probably.

"Soon there'll be—there'll be people coming through here, and it'll get out of hand—it'll be something you don't want to see . . ."

"Why *wouldn't* I want to see people?"

I'd dreamed of seeing people for twelve days . . .

He looked over at his comrades. Soldiers, on the road to nowhere. One of them turned, leaning from his truck window, and made a gesture to Starkey to hurry up. The vehicle had rounded the intersection up ahead.

"We're getting left behind!" the other guy yelled, and finally moved on, jogging after his friend and then climbing into the second truck.

Starkey turned to leave.

"Who are you?" I asked him.

"I'm nobody," he said as he held his rifle with both hands. "Just—just keep your head down, kid. Won't be long."

Won't be long? "What won't be long?"

He walked away. Square shoulders filling out his plastic parka. Hope departing. Just like that. No answer.

I ran after him. Fell into step beside him. His eyes scanned the street. The guy's expression was stone. He looked down at me like I was nothing. Like I, and all this around us, was too big a problem for one man and his buddies to deal with.

"Don't make me stay here," I pleaded, falling into step beside him, heading for the departing trucks. "There's thousands of those infected—"

"They won't last much longer," he said. "They'll become ill and worse due to injury and exposure, lack of nutrition, all that. They can't last long on just water . . ."

"No, you don't understand, there's another kind of infected—"

"I've seen, kid," he said, zipping his collar up tight against a horizontal snow drift. "There are two clear groups of the infected. Yeah? I've seen that. Those who are literally bloodthirsty killers, and those who are content with any liquid to survive. Either way, both groups need fluid constantly; got themselves some kind of psychogenic polydipsia, they *need* to drink. It's the *why* that bothers me—why the two *different* conditions . . ."

He seemed lost in the thought, a thousand-mile stare.

"That's why you're here?"

He eventually shrugged in reply.

"Maybe the ones who chase after people were already screwed up?" I said. "Murderers and criminals, stuff like that."

"Maybe, kid," he said, looking at his trucks. "But I doubt it."

"They're *driven* to kill for blood," I said urgently. "I've seen them. They prey on others, take advantage of them. They're getting stronger while the rest—the general population of infected—are getting weaker. The gap is growing bigger. The weak congregate, for safety maybe. They flock to where there's easy water, they make do. The strong are in smaller packs, plenty are doing it alone, and they're as strong as they were on day one, maybe even more so."

"The ones just drinking water will die out if they don't start getting some nutrients in them," Starkey said. "Hell, we've already seen plenty who hyper-hydrated to the point of fatal disturbance in brain functions."

"The others?"

"The others . . ." he shrugged. "Well, they might just be around forever."

3

"Where does that leave me?"

He kicked at an empty drink can in the snow, looking pained. "Just go," he said. "Soon as you can, whether you find your friend or not. Get out and don't stop until you find someplace safe."

When the explosion happened, I was full of homesickness for Australia. Would it be wrong to turn my back on New York now, when it needed me most? For all I knew Felicity was alone out here somewhere . . . could I just leave?

Was there anything left of New York to see before I went back? Dave said his parents lived somewhere out near Williamsburg. Maybe there was still time to go and see his folks, check on life beyond this island. To tell them what a mate he'd turned out to be in the end. Or was that part of my past, never to be revisited? I knew that to survive, I had to think of the future.

"Keep heading north," the man was saying. "Far as you can."

"Are you sure?"

"I sent my family to Canada. That's as sure as I can tell you I am."

"Canada's okay?"

"That's what I last heard."

"What about Australia?"

He slung his rifle over his shoulder, adjusted the strap, then put his hood on.

"Please," I said, "if you know something—"

He shrugged. "I've heard nothing beyond what's here and now in my backyard. That's a big enough problem for me. Just head for somewhere upstate at least. Hole up, find others, a town or somethin', safety in numbers. Keep off the major roads in your travels—there'll be more like us and worse."

He looked down at his feet, then across at his buddies in their big-wheeled trucks, now passing through the next intersection.

"Why north?" I asked. My breath fogged in front of me, fast jets of steam.

"This illness," he said, looking down at me, "it does better in the heat. Lives in the air, on the ground, stays active *longer*, stays *alive*, you understand?"

"No, not really." I didn't want to sound dumb, but I felt I had to know, whether or not he took me seriously enough to explain.

"The biological agent is still a threat, see? The cold kills it, it can't live without a host for long."

"How long?"

"I'm not sure. Days, less than a week."

I hoped a week would be long enough to find Felicity and the others, to persuade them to come with me. Safety in numbers, right?

"But we're leaving now," Starkey said, as if reading my thoughts.

Was that an offer?

"I can go and check on Felicity, if you wait here. I'll be quick."

He shook his head. "Can't take no baggage, sorry, kid. I gotta go."

I thought fast. Could I give up on my hope of finding Felicity—so fast, so easily? "If it's a problem to wait . . ."

I mean, could I even be sure that she actually existed, anyway? She could just be another illusion like Mini, Anna, and Dave. How could I trust myself after being alone all this time? Starkey hadn't looked as if he believed me, that's for sure. It'd be stupid to let this opportunity of rescue, of safety, to slip through my fingers because I'd run off to find someone who wasn't there.

Then again, if I found Felicity and came back, Starkey might not be here because he didn't exist either. But this had to be real, didn't it? I couldn't have made up what he was saying about the chemical agent. About all that noise and shooting just now . . .

I shook my head clear. No, Starkey was *real*. Felicity was *real*. The choice was *real*.

"Please, can't I come with you now?"

"*No.*"

I was about to argue the point when he grabbed the

front of my coat, held me, almost in the air. I waited for him to toss me to the ground or yell in my face.

"You find some other survivors like you 'round here like I said. You stick with them and head north, far as you can. You follow us and you're dead. Ain't nothin' more I can do for you, same as there ain't nothin' I can do to stop my guys from protecting themselves if they see you as a threat."

"That's why you can't take me?"

"That and more." Starkey put me down. I no longer thought any of them were really military guys—they didn't fit the part. American soldiers wouldn't leave me like this. They wouldn't look like this—uniforms, sure, but not with the different haircuts and weapons and stuff. His backpack was like the one I had for school. They looked about my dad's age or older.

But none of that mattered. None of them turned around. No one seemed to notice me, not even my guy Starkey. They left me standing there, alone.

4

So I followed them, carefully keeping out of their way. A block. Two. On the third, they stopped and sent one of the men ahead on foot. The next intersection was impassable, even for their heavy trucks. They could push vehicles aside, one by one, but here was what remained of a tall building, now a three-story mountain of jagged rubble, covering the street. There was a lot of arguing and pointing, as they looked at what must have been maps or aerial photographs to find another route to wherever they were headed.

I kept checking over my shoulder, but there was nothing, no Chasers. Wherever they were, they weren't out in the open today. But I still felt their presence, always there, lurking, watching, hunting.

The wind died down and it started to snow more heavily. Silent curtains of falling white powder. The clouds were dark. My neck and face were numb, my feet frozen. I sheltered in an alcove across the street and watched the convoy. They were shiny new monsters of things, jacked up on high suspension with chunky tractor tires eating into the snow. But the tops of the trucks—the hoods and canvas cargo covers—had been spray-painted white, for camouflage, I guess.

The men continued to argue among themselves. The driver of the second truck was guided by the driver of the first, who now stood on the roof of a crashed taxi, pointing to an easy path to clear.

The drivers got back into their cabs, and the first truck inched steadily forward, creating a path through the rubble mountain that seemed impassable from this vantage. Not even a couple of dozen cars and vans in the tangle could stop it from pushing on, its chunky tires never losing traction. They'd be through in maybe ten minutes. I'd forgotten the kind of power and freedom that a decent vehicle can provide. My twelve days of trekking and exploring had been limited to what I could achieve on my own two legs with the occasional help of a standard police car that I'd called my own.

While the first truck ploughed on, a couple of soldiers went into the lobby of a nearby office building, set up a propane burner, and put some water on the boil. Starkey crossed the street, headed my way, stopping a few paces before me. He was silent, as if he couldn't bring himself to tell me to beat it again. He pushed some snow off a bench and sat down.

The more time I spent with him, the less like a soldier he seemed. His eyes may even have been kind—they were not hard, not mean or evil.

"Thanks for before," I said, and sat next to him. "My name's Jesse."

He undid his coat's collar. "I don't want to know that."

He looked back at his buddies. One walked over, passing him a tin cup of steaming coffee. This soldier, short and stocky with big bloodshot eyes, was all anger, all simmering rage, keen to take the fight to someone. I knew that feeling.

I said to them, "Try heading west two blocks, then down—"

"If I wanted your opinion I'd have asked for it," the hostile guy snapped.

"I only—"

"You've got a big mouth, kid." He shot Starkey a look before walking back to his friends.

Starkey passed me his coffee. I turned it down and he said, "Not from around here, are you?"

I shook my head.

"You were here on holiday?"

"Something like that," I replied.

"Well, aren't you right out of luck."

"Where's the help?"

"You're lookin' at it."

"Serious?"

"Yep." He took off his gloves and placed them on the ground.

"Then I sure am out of luck."

He nodded, sipping the steaming brew through his thick gray moustache. The snow caught in his stubble and softened his appearance.

"There're some roadblocks farther up on the major arterials leading outta here; that's about as much a response to this as I've seen."

"Where's the government?"

"That's a million dollar question, kid," he said.

"So what about the roadblocks?" I said. Something shifted in my stomach: butterflies, excitement, possibility. "Does that . . . What does that mean?"

"Means roads in and out are blocked."

"But, it means other places are okay outside of New York?"

"No, kid, it's not just here. Like I said before." He looked up at the sky, squinted against the glare of the dull sun hiding behind a dull gray sky. "They're up there, too. Watching. Counting. Got drones and whatnot buzzing around. They're just trying to contain the worst of this wherever they can, see?"

No, I didn't. I had a million questions. "*You* got through. How'd you get here, onto Manhattan? The bridges are down, the tunnels are . . ."

He nodded.

"Because you guys are soldiers?"

He smiled. "I look like a soldier?"

"You're dressed like one."

"We found a way around," he said. "Wasn't easy, though. Trucks helped, guns too."

I tried asking again. "What are you doing here?"

"Doesn't matter."

"I don't think you'd risk being here if it didn't matter," I probed.

"I mean it doesn't matter to you."

Okay. It wasn't so much what he said as the way he said it. Everything mattered to me: any sign of life, any ray of hope. He wasn't going to understand that, though, not in the few minutes we had to talk. I imagined what it would be like to be in the back of their truck, protected. They'd do whatever they had to do here and then we'd all leave, go someplace where it was warm and the people were friendly and there would be news and answers.

"Is this war?"

"We've been at war for a while now," he said. He squinted at the demolished high-rise on the block and there was real anger there. "This is the next step. Difference is, the frontline is now here; right here on *our* doorstep."

Which war? On terror? In the Middle East?

His friends hollered to him. The break was over, they were moving out.

"Look, I gotta go," he said, slapping me on the shoulder, looking in my eyes like my dad had when he'd said good-bye to me at the airport. "Keep safe, kid. Keep your head down."

"No! Wait! So, this roadblock, it means there's heaps of uninfected out there?"

"Because of a roadblock? No." One glove, two. "Like I said, they're doing that to keep the worst of everything here in this place. You got a massive congregation here, millions of people packed dense, no telling what'd happen to small towns out there that might so far be uninfected if they—all these contaminants—get out of here."

I didn't like that he called them "contaminants." They were people. Sick, sure, but they didn't want to be that way. Their trucks started up again. So loud.

"But you can't catch this infection."

"What are you? A doctor?" he gave a sideways grin, tipping out the rest of his coffee onto the snow where it melted down to the pavement.

I was silent. He was right. How the hell was I sure you couldn't catch this? Because *I* hadn't? What if it was transferred from the infected through blood or saliva?

Plenty of diseases and viruses were passed like that. And maybe I was only safe because I hadn't been bitten yet. I'd thought the risk was over, that because I'd avoided catching the virus initially, I'd avoided it altogether.

"Think about it this way," he said. "No one's come in to fix this up yet, have they? So as big and serious as the situation is here, must be a lot worse elsewhere, yeah?"

It felt awful to hear him say what I'd been thinking. I sat there. Watching him leave, again. He wavered this time.

"You got a gun?" he asked me.

"Not with me."

"Want one?" he asked, showing me a small pistol holstered to his belt.

I shook my head. "I've survived until now, haven't I?"

"That you have," he said. He gave me a half-smile, and I couldn't help but feel somewhat better seeing it, the first real smile in twelve days.

I stared at the ground, trying to think of ways to stay talking to him, of somehow convincing him to let me tag along. I wouldn't be in their way. I could help them.

"For what it's worth," he said, "I knew as soon as I saw you."

"Knew what?"

"You're a survivor."

5

The weather eased and snow feathered down. I walked warily, always checking behind me, keeping in the middle of the street, clear from dark storefronts and what might hide within them, following the footsteps of the soldiers. For almost half an hour I ambled. The city was silent but for the diminishing hum of the trucks. The clouds grew dark. I passed countless billboards, advertising goods that were no longer for sale. I walked on, falling farther behind them, a lone rear guard.

The foreign, man-made rumble of engines had been music to my ears; now it was a fading sound and I didn't want it to end. It was the noise that kept me there in the soldiers' wake, and stopped me from returning to Central Park to find Felicity. It reminded me of how noisy I thought this city was when I first encountered it, how busy. Now, look: the American dream replaced by a nightmare for anyone left to witness it.

Starkey was walking out front of his group, scanning the way. Once, he turned around and saw me.

He didn't wave, didn't threaten, just clocked me and continued on.

There was gunfire from afar and it made them pause, made them look around all ways and—

A noise, near, to my right.

I looked at the row of storefronts—dark open mouths of broken glass and shadows. There was a disturbance coming from the one next to me: the sound of a falling can, the scrape and shuffling of deliberate movement.

I'd only taken a step backwards, just one, before a face appeared. Dark eyes peered at me from around the doorway, filled with the vacant gaze of the infected. It was a man who'd been reduced to a thirsty shell, with sunken cheeks and cracked lips, dried red blood around his mouth and down his neck.

A Chaser. The hunter kind.

He was tall, hunched over, imposing and inquisitive, and as he watched me he became more alert.

I didn't move.

He did.

He came out of the shop and stood on the sidewalk, watching me. Eyes only for me. I'd almost forgotten what these ones looked like up close. Nothing redeeming. His bare hands were black, hanging by his side, dead weights. His gaze took me in, read me, my fear. Then his expression shifted, as he realized what I had to offer and that he had a chance at it. He zeroed in on me, his intent clear, his decision made.

He came at me, a few steps and then a sprint. I backed away and slipped, crashing to the ground as the Chaser pounced, literally launching off his feet at me as I lay cowering.

CRACK! A gunshot rang out loud, echoing about the canyonlike streets.

The Chaser was blown back a few yards. He hit a wall, dead. His chest displayed a single hole; black-red-brown, so little blood, hollow, empty, dehydrated. He was still, motionless. Graveyard dead.

I remembered when I'd shot the Chaser out in front of 30 Rock. The noise of the gun going off had seemed too loud as it echoed around the empty streets of Midtown Manhattan. I'd looked at the Chaser and at the gun in my hand. Then I'd run to the gutter and thrown up.

A block up the street, my soldier friend coolly brought his rifle down, its barrel smoking. With neither a wave nor a word he turned and walked away.

Half an hour later when my heart had stopped pounding and the soldiers were long gone, I picked up my backpack from where I'd ditched it the day before: around the corner of West 73rd Street, off Broadway. I retrieved my jacket, too—a big FDNY fireman's coat—crumpled and stiff with cold. From the backpack I took out a bag of dried fruit and a bottle of juice, then I put the big jacket on over the puffy one I already wore, looped the bag's straps over my shoulders, clipped the fastener around my stomach, picked up my breakfast and started off, eastward.

My only clue as to Felicity's whereabouts was the spot in the park where we'd each seen Chasers around a fire. They may still be there, she may be with them. I imagined finding her and telling her everything I'd just learned from Starkey—it wasn't much, but it was a hundred percent more information than I'd had since this attack began.

Across the street, I stopped and turned around. I took it all in. A convenience store, its window cracked. I looked at myself in the reflection of the glass and moved closer, pushing my nose against the cold surface, seeing nothing but myself. I rested my weary head against the window and closed my eyes.

This was where I'd last seen Anna, Mini, and Dave; that final glance of broken friends through broken glass. It was here I'd said good-bye, taken off my back-pack and ran. I hadn't even bothered to take the gun from my bag—there had been too many Chasers after us and it would only have been good for one thing and I wasn't interested in that. The gun was still there, I felt it, in a side pocket, next to a little wind-up flash-light. I could reach them both now within a second, if I wanted to. Yesterday I'd stood right here on Broadway and ripped the bandages off my bloodied hands and attracted them, let them chase after *me*. Now this place was empty of life, not a Chaser to be seen.

Not even a full day had passed since saying good-bye and yet I struggled to think of what my friends looked like. If this was what just a few hours could do, what would I forget tomorrow? What would I have left by next week? I kept my friends alive in my heart but could no longer conjure their faces.

I opened my eyes and took a deep breath. The street around me was empty. What did I have now—a life with no one in it? A life with the possibility of finding Felicity, who I knew only from a tiny little video screen? What I wanted was company, what I needed was to get home. My life was about getting off this island—through that roadblock—and the possibility of finding Felicity gave me purpose. Since seeing Felicity's recording, I knew I'd made the right choice. I knew she would lead me home.

Inside, the store was dark and most of the shelves were bare. I took some canned food—soups, fruit, creamed rice—a couple of bottles of soft drink, some blocks of chocolate, a small box of cereal and some long-life milk. I zipped up my backpack, slipped it back on, and felt its weight.

I took the little wind-up flashlight from my backpack's side pocket, flicked it on and wound it up bright to look around on the floor in the back aisle. There was rotting food on the tiles, melting and stewing, and bags of frozen food ripped apart and plundered where they lay—dogs, maybe rats, had been here. I remembered hearing somewhere that Manhattan had like seventeen million rats for every person. Maybe it was a joke, but if that were true, it'd now be more like seventeen billion to one. Maybe they were swarming under the city, somewhere warm probably, smarter than me, thriving in this new world . . . I headed for Central Park.

6

The friendly Chasers were gone. Where they'd been, the ground was littered with empty plastic bottles—lumps sticking out from the snow, undisturbed since the overnight snowfall. All around me was just white-gray slush, not even a set of telltale footprints.

Had Felicity made contact with them and followed them somewhere? Or, if she hadn't, why hadn't she returned to her home last night? On that little video screen she'd looked fit, healthy, capable. Surely if she was okay she would have gone back home. You'd run through the rain and dust and ash—you'd stop at nothing to be with your friends and family, even if all you had left were the remainders of them in an empty home.

A steel drum was overturned. I looked in it—ash. I took off a glove and felt the drum. It was cold, but not freezing cold, like the fire had gone out overnight, just a few hours before. I rolled the burned-out shell a few times, unsettling its black-gray contents, and looked inside at a tiny glowing ember. I thought about taking it out, putting it in my pocket, having its warmth travel with me, but if they returned, they'd need it more than me.

Maybe they'd simply run out of fuel or drink—I could see neither nearby—and gone on a re-supply trip. They could soon be back with more supplies. Or perhaps they'd set up camp at the next spot that provided what they needed, and they'd keep moving on like that. Either way, there was nothing here for me now.

I stood, leaving their things behind with a final look, and began walking east, towards the sun. Exiting the park, I passed thick shrubbery and saw the back of a still figure. Sleeping once, now covered in snow and ice, long lost into a never-ending dream. I approached slowly and retched when I saw the bloodstains. I rolled the body over with my foot. Its head was featureless, its face gnawed away, the miniature work of rats or some other scavenger.

That will never happen to me, no matter what.

I followed the tire tracks of the soldiers' trucks, black grooves in the pristine white landscape down to the ash on the blacktop. At the corner of Fifth Avenue, I stopped under the awning of the Plaza Hotel. The tracks turned south and soon became impossible to see. Looking north, the shattered remnants of everything in this street were disappearing in the driving snow. Visibility was no more than a block in either direction.

This was not a day for exploring or being trapped out in the elements. I needed someplace safe, somewhere close.

Across the street, the Pulitzer Fountain was dark, full of black water. Snow was falling hard now. My face was cold, my feet were freezing. The wind around my ears made me feel that at any moment there could be someone coming up behind me. I could never shut out thoughts like that.

The doors of the Plaza were locked, shin-deep snow had drifted up against them. It was dark inside. The only signs of human intervention since the attack were marks on the doors, and on the buildings on the opposite corner. Large spray-painted Xs, with numbers and letters in each quadrant, seemed to record some kind of coded information. I heard a gunshot, far-off, then a few more in quick succession.

A group of people were coming down Fifth Avenue, moving dark silhouettes, barely visible amidst the snow shower. Six of them. I watched them as they neared me. The soldiers? No. Chasers. Time to move away. I stayed low, keeping against the cars and buildings, and moved up Fifth Avenue.

There was a pile of rubble up ahead. The figures had stopped in the street, about where I had been standing. Above them was a building with a ten-story billboard running down its side: a woman dressed in not much, advertising . . . a handbag, I think. Despite its size it was hard to tell for sure; hard to imagine a time when anything about that ad made sense.

I jogged north up Fifth, holding my coat collar tight

around my neck to keep the wet out, huddling to the right, sticking close to the buildings for shelter. They were still there behind me, still coming, and matching my speed. I knew they'd not yet seen me, otherwise they'd be chasing hard. They were following my footprints, fresh in the snow. I started to run, flat out, giving everything I had.

The roads here looked no different from the sidewalks—they were all covered in smashed and crashed cars and vans and trucks, everything buried in ice and snow and ash and debris—and now rain. Up ahead was the mountain of rubble strewn across the road, impassable. I was pretty sure I'd watched this very building come down from the observation deck at 30 Rock in those first few days; a cloud of dust and ash in the still air. Ragged, dangerous.

I had three options: go around the rubble and through the likely dangers of Central Park, find my way eastward around the next block or two and probably encounter more of the same impassable ruins, or go back the way I'd come.

I looked back at the figures. They'd stopped momentarily, but started up again no sooner than I'd recounted the six of them. They moved more quickly this time, running hard—then two peeled off down a side street.

I went with my first choice, and ran across the road to the Central Park side. There was a building set inside the park, brick with white timber-framed windows, set down a couple of flights of steps from street level. It was big and regal looking; four or five stories high, with towers at the corners like some sort of castle. It looked undamaged, safe, and secure.

To my right there was a stone pillar supporting the steel handrail that led down the stairs. Set into the pillar was a green copper sign that read "To the Zoo and Cafeteria." I held onto the handrail and walked down the steps, slippery underfoot, icy slick, descending as quickly as I dared. I rushed towards the doors, which were set at the top of a short flight of stone stairs. I was scared and it was raining and I was cold. I shouldn't have come here, not today, not now.

Even if those Chasers overshot me, there might not be time in the daylight to make it somewhere safe to spend the night. I could see the Chasers up at street level, closing in; they were following my tracks just as they had been since the Plaza. Maybe the rain would wash them away just enough . . .

The front doors were brass-framed with clear glass inserts. They were locked. I stood still and listened. I could not hear anything, but I could see the tops of heads walking up the last block on the street up above. I had two minutes, max. Maybe I could smash the glass and unhook a latch or something? I cupped my hands around my eyes and peered through the door, trying to make out details through the glass. It was too dark. I squinted, scanned around, trying to make sense of it.

My own eyes stared into mine, wide, still, spooked. But then they moved. I hadn't moved. The eyes I saw were not mine—someone was there, inside, looking back at me.

7

Her name tag read "Rachel." She looked about my age, but was small and slight. She watched me tap on the doors, pleading to get in. She stared out at me, stunned, but not with the vacant expression that I'd grown so used to seeing on Chasers. I saw fear in her eyes, not thirst: here was another survivor.

I could understand if she was frightened. Maybe I was the first person she'd seen since the attack. Or maybe she was in charge of a group of survivors, and was unwilling to risk their safety by admitting a stranger. I mightn't look like someone you'd want to get close to—hell, I'd been surprised at my own reflection these past few days. I no longer looked like *me*. I was a different me—one who could hold a gun and shoot, one who had mastered the art of self-preservation. The cut on my eyebrow from when I hit my head in the subway carriage after the explosion had healed, but it had left an angry scar. My hair and clothes were sodden from the rain. My skin was pale and drawn across my features.

"Please!" I mouthed to her. "Please, let me in?" I rattled the doors.

Then she moved. Just a little, just enough to give me hope.

"Can I come in?" I called into the crack where the two doors met. I stood back and forced a smile, my hands up in the air to show I was getting wetter and colder out here, that I was harmless.

She did not respond.

"Rachel," I said, indicating her name badge. "My name's Jesse. Are you—are you okay?"

Her gaze shifted; she was looking over my right shoulder. I turned in that direction.

Up at street level, the group of four Chasers was almost at the top of the stone stairs. I dared not make a sound. A couple were preoccupied with the falling rain, heads tilted skyward, their insatiable thirst being met by the heavens. They walked past the stairs, didn't even look my way. Maybe they'd missed my tracks heading down here? I didn't move until they were out of sight. Wet snow ran down the back of my neck.

I turned back to the door—Rachel was gone. I walked back down the stairs and ran around the side of the building. There was a sign that read "New York State Arsenal, Erected 1848." No wonder it looked so imposing; a fortress in the middle of the city.

I imagined that there was a refuge inside—that Rachel was one of many survivors here, with the zoo workers and their friends and families. They'd have hot food and answers and laughs. Maybe I could stay here with them until rescuers arrived. I could help with the animals, collect food from nearby abandoned stores and apartments.

Or Rachel could join me in finding Felicity, and the three of us could leave the city together, and head north.

Looking around, I tossed my backpack over a tall metal fence, heaved myself up and over it, and landed heavily on the other side. There were several other brick buildings behind this imposing arsenal, covered and semi-covered walkways linking them, a big pool in the center.

"Hello?" I called, as loud as I dared. I could not see anyone, and I could not hear anything but the icy rain hitting hard surfaces and buildings around me, the snow underfoot turning to slush. "Rachel?"

I opened a door to a building marked as a cafeteria. "Anyone here?"

No answer. Empty. No sign of life.

I started to feel uneasy. What if there were no group of survivors here, no Felicity to be found nearby, just Rachel? I couldn't help but feel a little stab of disappointment at the thought of having to make do with this unresponsive, cautious girl. But I *had* to give her a chance. Give us both a chance.

I approached another door at the rear of the arsenal building. It was ajar.

"Hello?" I called inside as I pushed it open. Rachel was in the shadows, alone, at the far end of a hallway at the bottom of some stairs. "Hi. Can I please—"

"I don't have anything." Her voice was squeaky, shaky.

"There's that shovel," I said.

She looked at the makeshift weapon in her hands, then back to me.

I said, "I'm not the enemy."

"Are you sick?"

"No."

"You're sure?"

"Yes."

She looked around to the side of the building, and then back at me.

"Did you just jump the fence?"

"Yeah."

She almost looked impressed, but didn't say anything more. I recognized she was more than just scared or cautious; she was alone here. Just her and the animals.

I needed a way of breaking the ice, to get her to trust that I meant her no harm.

"Hey, you wouldn't be missing a polar bear, would you?"

She came forward, two, three steps, considering me more now. I could see up close that she was probably only a year or two older than me—there was a young, pretty face under all that grime and exhaustion.

"You saw a polar bear? Where? When?" Her head tilted to the side, her eyes watched me, closely.

"A few nights ago. Near the library, 42nd and Fifth?"

"Oh . . ." she said, seeming disappointed by that, either the timing or the place. "Was he— Did he look okay?"

"Yeah," I said, trying to sound upbeat. "He was

sniffing around in the snow. More interested in finding food than in me. Seemed happy enough."

"He was alone?"

"Yeah, I just saw one," I said. "He mooched around
then ambled off."

The memory made me smile. Maybe if I told
Rachel more about that unexpected encounter, she
would realize I was on her side—on the side of the
animals too.

"I was spooked at the noises he was making," I continued, "but then when I saw him—I felt safe having
him around. Like he and I were in this together. I
threw him some fruit but he wasn't interested. He
seemed to prefer being on his own."

I remembered thinking that the polar bear might
sniff out the Chasers for us, warn us if they were coming. It might even keep them away. But it seemed
wrong to say that, to think of using him as a line of
defense. I didn't think Rachel would see polar bears
like that.

She smiled faintly, more with her eyes than her
mouth.

"How many were there?" I asked.

"Two," she said.

"Well, I'm sure they're both doing fine. So, where's
the rest of the zoo staff?" I asked, not wanting to let
on that I'd so quickly recognized her solo status.

"You're looking at it," she said, moving out towards
the zoo grounds. I put my backpack down by the back
door and followed her at a distance of a few paces. I
watched her do her chores. She delivered a bucket of

food to the penguins—tiny blurs of black and white that seemed oblivious to everything—then stopped and threw a toy back into the sea lions' enclosure.

"What happened to the others?"

"I wish I knew." She struggled to heave a sack of grains and wouldn't let me help her.

"You seem young to be—"

"I'm older than you."

"Okay. I didn't mean . . ." I hadn't meant to offend her. If anything, I'd meant it as a compliment. But maybe she was already tired of being the responsible one, dependable.

"I'm here on an internship, in my second year of vet school, from Boston. And I'm the only one who stayed here after the attack or whatever. That enough of a catch-up for you?"

I nodded. "Like I said, I'm Jesse. It's good to meet you."

She didn't shake my offered hand, didn't put the shovel down. "What's your accent?" she asked.

"I'm Australian."

She shrugged, as if she wasn't really interested. Silence as she worked, broken by a sudden banging at the front doors. Hard, rough, rattling.

"Who is it?" she asked. "Friends of yours?"

"I have no friends," I said, reality hitting me when I said this out loud. No point denying that anymore.

"Did you tell anyone you were coming here?"

"Everyone I know in this city is dead." That enough of a catch-up for her?

I followed her to the back doors, out of sight from those at the front of the building. "It's the Chasers."

"The what?" She looked across the doorway at me.

"The *who*. The infected."

"They don't bang on doors."

"These ones do more than that," I said. "These ones hunt."

That seemed to register. She shook her head, as if in denial, and bent down, moving slowly on her hands and knees into the doorway between us. I followed. The rattling had stopped. We crouched in the shadows, peered around a corner of the stairs to the doors at the end of the hall. Two Chasers were there, standing at the entrance, clearly looking for me. I'd led them here.

"I've put you in danger."

"Probably," she whispered. "I haven't seen these ones up close before."

"I have," I said. "I've seen them right up close. For keeps."

"They're . . ."

"Scary?"

"Intriguing." Rachel seemed genuinely fascinated by the Chasers. As if they were some new species of animal. "They don't seem that dangerous. They can't climb the fences, for one thing."

"Don't give them the chance to prove otherwise."

"So what do we do?" she demanded.

"We hope they leave." It was all I could think to say.

8

We made our way along the hall, keeping to the shadows and watching as the Chasers joined another pair at the foot of the stairs leading up to Fifth Avenue. One turned and looked back, but we may as well have been invisible from where we were hiding. Another two figures I guessed to be the ones who had peeled off from the group a few minutes earlier appeared at the top of the stairs at street level. They must have called or signaled down to their comrades, for the four of them climbed the stairs fast and disappeared down Fifth Avenue.

"What brought you here?" Rachel asked as we wandered back into the zoo grounds from the rear of the arsenal building.

"Being chased by those guys," I replied.

"Sure, but chased from where?"

"Near the Plaza Hotel, after I'd gone searching through another section of the park."

"What were you searching for in the park?"

"A girl."

She looked at me, smiled, and shook her head like I was nuts. I followed her to the locked door of a storeroom. Inside was dim, lit by snow-covered skylights, but she navigated with ease and passed me a couple of buckets of feed, which I could hardly lift. I followed her out.

"So you went out there in the park, with these—Chasers, you call them?—around, to look for a girl."

"Yep. A girl from a video."

"You don't even know her?"

"Nope."

"And you didn't find her?"

"Nope."

"Well, Jesse, at least I know now that you're a little crazy and reckless."

"I don't regret it, though," I said. "At least I found you."

As the afternoon grew darker and I continued to follow her around, Rachel remained wary, always keeping a safe distance, as if she might have to make a run for it at any moment. I found I liked just being around her, being around someone nonthreatening, residing in the comfort of our community of two. I hoped that she'd learn to share in that.

"You sure I can't do anything more to help?" I couldn't think of how to reassure her other than by proving myself by doing chores.

"This is my job, I have to do this. These animals—I'm all they have."

I got that. But couldn't I do something beyond lugging a few buckets? I kept a lookout, figuring maybe she would like me hanging around for that.

She checked on the penguins and the puffins and the sea lions who watched us closely. I saw she looked sad, worn out, beat. She finally stopped to rest and asked for my help in carting some water.

"I mean," Rachel said, out of breath, sinking onto a bench, "if you're just going to keep following me around . . ."

I used two large buckets, making trip after trip between the tap and the huge enclosed building that housed the tropical birds. After about ten minutes, Rachel joined me, lugging one bucket at a time.

On one trip I saw a sign for the polar bear enclosure. I wondered about sharing that vision I'd had of a new earth—a future where some kind of garden would secretly be growing up through the ruined ice rink, ready for the polar bear's return. He'd be king again, maybe start a family. But would that seem crazy to Rachel, who was coping with the day-to-day business of keeping the animals in her care alive? What did her idea of the future hold?

We were taking the water to the Tropic Zone, where inside it was warmer, a kind of big greenhouse island in a sea of snow. Hydrodynamic-something-or-other heating . . . My dad would know; he'd designed it into our house back home. It was some kind of system where heat was brought up from the ground in fluid-filled tubes and fed into the concrete slab floor to radiate the earth's natural heat. That, along with all the glazing that trapped what little sunlight there was, would be what warmed this place.

"Passive solar," she said, following my gaze up to the roof. It had an aluminum foil-type section in the middle with massive skylights; big angled windows that caught every ray of daylight. "There are solar panels on the roof too. They power the heating pumps. We wouldn't have been able to survive this long without them."

I liked that she referred to her family—her and the animals—as "we." Whatever was coming in the days ahead, there was a future right here.

"What are you smiling at?" she asked me as we stopped and caught our breath.

"Nothing," I said. My grin wasn't disappearing and neither was her look. "It's just nice to be useful."

Rachel nodded and went back to the colorful birds. One was an orange so vivid, I could not imagine it appearing in nature. It let her pet him while it stood there, pecking at the food.

"What is he?"

"A scarlet ibis," she said. He waddled along a branch and preened himself some more, oblivious to how the world had changed outside his enclosure.

"So, you've been studying veterinary science or something?" I asked.

"Yeah. I come from a family of doctors, but that wasn't for me."

"You like animals more than people?"

"Maybe," she said. "Animals are easier than people and a lot more reliable. And as much as I've cared for these guys here for the past two weeks, they've saved me too." She nodded, and another small crack appeared in her standoffish demeanor.

It made sense, summed her up; explained how she could go on caring for this menagerie. Rachel's fondness for the birds was mutual. And like her, they were keeping themselves busy, picking and preening, never still.

I followed her around some more, helped her repair a fence at the back of the zoo, carted more water until my arms felt like they'd fall off, then watched as she launched a bucket of meat into the snow leopard enclosure. We stayed there, leaning against the fence, watching them eat. It was getting dark, and the wind had picked up.

"Chocolate and Zoe," she said, detached, as the cats crunched on bones. "They were my primary job—I was one of their keepers."

"And now you're everyone's keeper."

Rachel nodded, the concept not lost on her; I think she liked that I got it. She looked at the big cats and they sometimes looked back at her. "They're why I'm still here," she said, quietly. Then she started to cry. "Long as it's just me here . . . they're why I can never leave."

9

I understood Rachel's feeling of responsibility for the animals, but it played no part in my plans to escape this city. Would I be wasting my time trying to get her to change her mind and to leave with me? I needed to find Felicity. She seemed so full of hope on the video, so determined to escape the dangers we were in. Maybe she could change Rachel's mind.

By evening, there was still some distance between Rachel and me, but I noticed she'd slowed and was showing none of the urgency and drive I'd seen in her earlier. We went inside and I shut the glass doors behind me. It was still cold, but thankfully the wind was shut out. Rachel locked the doors, bolts at the top and bottom.

"You'd better stay here tonight," she said as I followed her upstairs. "Bathroom's there," she said, pointing down the hallway. "Do you mind using a bucket—to flush, wash, whatever?"

"It's okay, I'm used to it," I said.

· Rachel led me into an office, the timber floor of the historic building creaking underfoot. There was a big old couch, which she'd obviously been using as a bed, a couple of windows with the curtains drawn, and an open fireplace. I looked at her little makeshift bed, the food, the small stack of clothing, the bottles of drink—all of it enough for one to survive for a short while and not much more. I took off my coat and wet shoes.

"I'll get the fire going," she said.

There was an old fireplace behind where the desk had recently been, a huge old leather-topped timber construction that was now pushed against a wall, leaving telltale dents of its former position in the ornamental carpet. The coals in the hearth glowed dull through black ash and charcoal. Rachel stoked them back to life with a poker, put on a fresh split log from the big steel bucket of firewood and coal briquettes that stood nearby. She waited a bit for the wood to spark, blew to coax them to ignite, then rose and lit an oil lamp on the desk, the type with a wick and a glass bell and little dial for adjusting brightness. Her face was friendly in that light.

"Sorry, Jesse," she said, pointing at an assortment of tubs, jars, packets, and cans on the desk. "I don't have much food to offer you—not much variety, nothing exciting. Just what I could keep from the cafeteria."

"I've got some food," I said, producing everything I had in my bag. "Soup?"

"Sure," she said, taking a pot and can opener from the desk. I set up my wind-up flashlight against a wall in the corner, so that it shone up to the ceiling like an up-light. I emptied two cans of chicken and vegetable soup into the pot and set it in the corner of the fireplace, nestled onto a bed of glowing coals. Rachel took off her polar-fleece sweatshirt, revealing just a T-shirt. Her arms were much skinnier than mine.

She looked at me, ran the back of her gloved hand across her sweaty forehead.

"So, you were here on vacation?" she asked.

"It was a UN leadership thing."

"The UN? As in the United Nations?"

"Yeah."

"No wonder there's problems . . ."

"What?"

"I mean, you seem a bit young for the UN."

I laughed. "Camp," I replied. "It was a senior school camp."

I told her about how I was on the subway when the attack on the city happened. How I'd gone to 30 Rock to see what I could of the city from the viewing platforms.

Everything I'd seen. I told her about Dave, Anna, and Mini. All I'd been through with them "by my side."

"That's . . . a special story."

"Yeah," I nodded in agreement.

She was being friendly, but I realized that special didn't really explain how I felt. I was sad to realize that, despite everything I'd done to hang on to them, I had been losing my friends gradually from the start.

Was I to blame for deceiving myself? Nobody had forced me to spend twelve days in total denial of the facts. All that time I'd been torn between wanting to leave and wanting to hide and wait until whatever had happened was over, and everything went back to normal. What could I have achieved if I'd accepted the truth the moment I woke up in the smashed train carriage? I wouldn't be here with Rachel, that was for sure. And I wouldn't have found the video of Felicity. There was a sacrifice to be made, however I looked at it.

I told Rachel as much as I knew about Felicity; that she was out there, somewhere, as of yesterday afternoon.

"She's lasted this long," Rachel said. "She's probably still okay, just had to shelter someplace else."

"I hope so."

"And it was this morning when you left hers?"

"Yeah."

"Well, it's only a day. She'll be all right."

She put a pot of water to one side of the fire.

"So," I asked, broaching a subject that I knew might well bring her some unwanted memories, "where were you when the attack on the city happened?"

"I was in the basement," Rachel said, her eyes reflecting the red of the embers. "I heard the explosions; they went on for about half an hour. I wasn't here in 2001, but I assumed it was terrorists again; that they'd come to finish the job, right?"

I shrugged, not knowing what to say. I'd come to my own conclusion that this was surely the work of some kind of nation-state rather than a group of crazy nut jobs, but I reminded myself that Rachel had not seen the scale of the destruction beyond the walls and fences of this zoo.

"When the explosions started, they evacuated the tourists and nonessential staff, and the rest of us went down to the basement. We stayed down there for hours, I didn't want to leave, but my colleagues helped me," she said, smiling but looking distant as she conjured the memories. "And when we finally did come back up, that's when we saw them, the . . . Chasers?"

"Yeah."

"Well, we saw them, deranged people, chasing people later in the day—on Fifth Avenue, and in the park. Didn't know what to make of it. With a few other staff I kept attending to the animals. My last coworkers left in the afternoon, after they'd tried for hours to contact their families and friends. Landlines, cell phones, TV and radio, all went out around the time of the attack. No one knew what had happened. Said they'd be back with help and security, but, well . . ."

"It's the same everywhere I've tried, too," I said, recognizing her frustration and resentment at being abandoned like that. "Every type of phone, all the television channels: blank. All the radio stations are either static or make a strange woodpecker sound. I think I heard some music on a car radio once, but I was tired and . . . I might have imagined it."

10

The thought of Rachel here by herself for twelve days, having little idea what was going on outside these walls, made me shudder. I adjusted the wood in the fire to avoid the burning log spilling out the grate. I was glad when she broke the silence and changed the subject.

"Whereabouts in Australia are you from?" It was nice to hear her ask a question like this. After the afternoon's silent chores, I was afraid that maybe she was too shell-shocked by all this destruction to talk much about anything beyond survival.

"Melbourne," I replied. "It's way down south—"

"I went there with my family when I was about your age," she said. She was thoughtful for a moment. "Nice place. Only spent a couple of days in Melbourne, though. We went to Sydney, mostly, and the outback."

"Where are you from?"

"Amarillo, Texas, originally. Moved to the West Coast when I was in junior high."

I listened to her talk about her old hometown. I asked her about cowboys and oil, she told me about her family and music, and we talked about being away from home and the things we missed. I liked Radiohead and Muse, she liked Kings of Leon and Green Day. We'd both learned some piano, liked to sing in the shower, and wondered why no one ever really became a real-life superhero.

"Yeah, like that *Kick-Ass* character."

"Exactly," she said, dipping a cracker into her steaming soup and savoring it. "Where's our Hit Girl and Big Daddy? Hell, where're our Guardian Angels?"

"Were those the guys who used to go around keeping the peace on New York subways?"

"They're still operating in some places apparently," she said. "Least, they were . . . Don't you wonder where the military is? Where's our police, our government?"

I finished my story from before, filling her in on my past twelve days and concluding with the day's events on the street, the trucks of soldiers and all that I could remember Starkey telling me.

"And these soldiers, did he tell you where they were going?"

"Wouldn't say," I replied. "But . . . they weren't like regular soldiers."

"What do you mean?"

"They were more like . . . renegade soldiers, unofficial or something. Older, like our parents' age. And one of the trucks had a big container in it," I said, thinking back. "Kind of the size of a big fridge. It had USA-something stenciled on it, and it looked military, too."

"I guess that makes sense about the roadblocks," she said. "Maybe they were a small scouting party, an advance unit that's the vanguard of a bigger relief effort or something."

"Yeah, but the weird thing was, the guy I spoke with said that they found a way *around* the roadblock."

"Around?"

"Yeah. I remember thinking the way he said it was strange, like they weren't meant to be here."

"And they didn't tell you what happened?"

I shook my head. "I told you everything he told me."

Telling her and seeing her reactions was reassuring; it seemed like it all made sense to her, at least a lot more sense than it made for me.

I tried to eat more slowly, and held back a laugh.

"What is it?"

"Not used to eating with company," I explained. "I—I've cooked and eaten pretty well, but guess I've grown used to just smashing it down fast."

"That's okay."

"I just . . . I guess learned to get by as best I could. I kept myself busy—exploring the building, making a sign on the roof, scanning the streets and horizons for hope."

"It's good to keep busy."

"Like you've done here. I think that's what got me through. That and luck."

"We've both been lucky," she said, pouring a couple of mugs of Coke and passing me one. "This was all up in the top floors of the GE Building at 30 Rock?"

I nodded. "Thanks." We clinked mugs. Her eyes glowed in the warm light of the fire.

"No other survivors there?"

"No one else I saw," I said. "You never know though, right? Someone may have locked themselves away in their apartment or office, waiting it out, waiting for help or death, whichever came first."

"That's what I've assumed is going on out there," she said. "I just assumed—I thought you would have seen lots of others."

"It's . . . it's just me. Do you have family here in Manhattan?" I asked quietly, over the steam of the soup.

"No," she replied. "Most of my family's in southern California. I've been here for three and a half months. I live by myself in Williamsburg—that's just across the East River."

I crunched my cracker and sipped my soup.

"I couldn't feed them," she said suddenly.

"Sorry?"

"The polar bears. I didn't have enough for them and everyone else . . . I had to let them out."

I felt as though she thought I was judging her, her work, her decisions.

"They'll be okay," I said. "It's winter—they can stick to the snow and head north, head home . . ."

"I actually envy them that," Rachel said.

"Their strength?"

"In a way, yeah: to be strong enough, equipped

with the innate ability to get out there in this harsh environment and find a way home. Hundreds or thousands of years of our species being soft and lazy makes it difficult for us to do much of anything out there."

The weather rattled against the curtained window. It was good to eat with company, but eating seemed like a chore to Rachel, like she forced herself to have something to keep her energy up—if she faltered, if she failed, all the animals would suffer her fate. She sat cross-legged, her empty cup in her hands, watching the wood burn.

"You happy to sleep there?" she said, pointing to the stack of blankets I sat on.

"Sure," I said. I made a bed of them, switched off my flashlight, climbed in and took off my damp clothes. She hung my jeans and shirt over a chair by the hearth, taking care as she did so and not saying a word. "Thanks."

She knelt by the fire, poking at the coals, put a big thick log on and went to her own bed. The lamp went out and I watched the flickering of the orange light from the flames and the shadows they cast on the ceiling. I was warm and cozy in this little room, more so than at any moment I could remember.

"I can stay and help you, if you like?" I said. Rachel was silent, but I knew she was awake and had heard me. "Or . . . if I find Felicity, and we, I mean, if you want to, maybe we can all try to escape Manhattan . . ."

I knew my words were pointless, knew that nothing I could say would persuade this girl to leave her animals alone and defenseless. I'm sure some part of her wanted to be at home, but how could she leave? What would it take?

The silence between us lasted until I was drifting off. I'd thought she was asleep, but when my new friend spoke her voice was clear and alert and showed that she felt and thought more about the situation than I'd allowed.

"It won't make much difference what we do," she said. "None of it makes much difference. We're stuck here, stuck with what we've got."

11

The morning was bright and my eyelids were heavy. I rolled from my side to my back and stared up at the ceiling. For a moment I forgot where I was. I'd slept well, by far the best sleep I'd had these past thirteen days.

It was a quarter-past nine. I stretched out, my back aching from this too-short makeshift bed. Just a few more minutes of sleep. I let myself doze, then sat up with a start, feeling sick. Twenty-past nine! I jumped up. I had to get to Rockefeller Plaza, to be there on time in case Felicity showed.

All my clothes felt dry as I pulled them on and Rachel had laid out a clean T-shirt and hooded jumper next to my jeans. I noticed there were a dozen or so radios on the table; walkie-talkie type things for the zoo staff to communicate with each other. I tried them all, but the batteries were dead.

Some cereal and long-life milk were set out, but I left the breakfast untouched. I put two radios in my backpack as well as a charging unit. I'd take them to 30 Rock, charge them up. Rachel needed a generator here, and I'd bring her one of those as soon as I could. I pulled on my shoes and ran downstairs, my backpack over one shoulder.

Rachel was in an enclosure feeding and watering some monkeys. I watched, silent, hopping from one foot to the other and unsure whether I should interrupt. I waited for her to come out.

"You're heading off?" she asked as she walked by, seemingly too preoccupied with the morning's work to stop and chat. She didn't sound surprised.

"For a bit," I said, running to catch up with her.

She stood up, wiped her brow, and hefted a big tub containing sad-looking fruit and vegetables, chopped and broken and sprouting here and there. She added a scoopful to a bucket, hesitated, then added a little more.

"When will their food run out?"

"Four days for the big cats," she said. "Not long after for the other carnivores—sea lions will run out in six or seven days. Rest have maybe a couple of weeks' worth."

"Right," I said. "I'm on it."

Now I had surprised her. She couldn't hide it from her voice. "On it?"

"I'll bring back food," I said, zipping up my coat. "As much as I can carry."

"I don't expect you to do that."

"How else will they eat?"

She looked at me, paused at the entrance to the tropical bird enclosure, and put the feed bucket down. "You're serious?"

"Sure!" I said. I slipped the backpack properly across both my shoulders. "I'm headed out anyway, and they need food."

"You're going right now?"

I checked my watch, nodded.

"You're going to look for that girl?"

"I left her that note."

"But what if—" A worried look passed over her face. She'd seemed certain that Felicity would be okay, so who was she worried about—herself, the animals? Or me? I couldn't work it out.

"I'll come back this afternoon," I replied. I knew what she had been going to say: *What if she doesn't show?* Maybe even some version of, *What if she's dead?* "I'll bring back as much food as I can find."

Rachel nodded, and I stepped forward and hugged her. She didn't move, and she felt so small in my arms. I moved back. She didn't have an expression other than exhaustion, and she went back to work. I didn't mind if she didn't believe me, I was just looking forward to seeing her reaction when I returned with another survivor and more food for her animals than she could have imagined.

Twenty minutes later I was at the corner of Fifth Avenue and East 57th. The skyscraper that had stood on the corner, between 57th and 56th, had come down, blocking the intersection entirely. It must have collapsed last night—there was no snow on the debris, but it was ankle-deep on the ground all around it. There was occasional movement as rubble shifted. I looked through some of the wreckage. There was a bent mail trolley that wouldn't push straight; a leather couch that stood on its side, not a scratch on it; a smashed television; an unbroken wineglass; a dismembered foot, as white as the snow.

I backtracked east to get around, moving fast, keeping to the center of the road so I'd have time to run from any Chasers that might leap out of a dark storefront. I stopped at the next block. There was money blowing from a bank's open door, a steady stream of worthless paper.

I scanned the road for footprints. The snow here was virginal: light, fluffy, a Styrofoam landscape under the winter's morning sun. I looked north and south along Avenue of the Americas. There was a whistling or sucking sound, constant but faint. Wind through broken buildings, maybe. I pressed on, walked out to the middle of the next white intersection, the snow crunching loudly underfoot. Blinding white and contrasting dark shadows in each direction. I turned south—

The ground beneath me gave way.

My feet fell through the snow—my legs, my waist, my chest disappeared down a hole in the street. My chest hit hard, knocking the wind from me. I flung my arms forward, my hands dug into the snow, clawed at it, fighting for breath.

I was sliding down, down into a hole in the road that had been iced and snowed over, cloaked in an invisibility blanket. I tried to hold on, to get any kind of grip to slow my descent, but my gloved fingers were sliding through loose snow on frozen ground, my feet dangling into what I imagined was an open manhole. When it was just my head above the ground level, my hands lost all purchase. I fell into the darkness.

12

The wind whistled around me. A shaft of sunlight penetrated the gloom as snow poured softly from the street level above. I could have been in a giant hourglass, the sands of time set to drown me.

This was no manhole.

I had landed on a steeply tilted ledge, a large chunk of broken road hanging by pipes, but I was slowly slipping down, deeper underground, the street level getting farther and farther from my reach.

Below me was a subway tunnel—I saw the glinting tiles of a platform, illuminated by the shaft of daylight above me, the howling of the wind as it whipped through like an express train. The next fall would hurt.

I grabbed hold of an edge of the asphalt, on my side, my feet hanging off the bottom edge. I tried pulling myself up, but my handhold gave way, a chunk of road-base crumbling away, and my fingertips and palms ground along the snow-covered surface. I was falling again, moving fast and hard through open space.

The impact of landing knocked the air out of me and I could hardly breathe. I was flat on my back, winded, my near-empty backpack having broken my fall. My chest felt tight, crushed. Something sharp bit into the back of my leg—I sat up quickly, alert.

It was dark all around but for the shaft of daylight in which I sat, as if I were at the bottom of a crumbling well. Snow from above whipped around in the wind and stung my eyes. I crawled into the shadows and listened.

Amidst the sound of the gale ripping through the tunnel I could hear dripping water, what seemed like a constant stream of run-off into a pool. Slowly my eyes adjusted and revealed a little more around me— the walls were white and I could pinpoint where the sound of wind was coming from, passing through the tunnels, being sucked out through another hole in the street above. When I shifted farther I could see there was the faint glow of daylight to my left.

But it didn't feel right down here. Didn't smell right.

I slipped my pack off my back, as quietly as I could, and fumbled with the side zipper. My hands felt raw, one glove had fallen off and the bandages beneath were ripped. I found my wind-up flashlight. I flicked the switch but the dull illumination did little, so I wound the handle to build the charge and it shone brightly.

A mass of people were crowded around, all turning as one to stare at my light.

Chasers.

Their faces were pale and ghostlike and they all looked my way. There were a hundred at least, sitting and standing on the subway platform, and more huddled on the tracks. All of them were staring at the light, staring at me. I scrambled to my left, flashlight in one hand and backpack in the other.

I stumbled and bumped into a Chaser—another one, a wall of them. They were blocking my path, but I pushed through them and towards the faint glow of daylight at a far wall. I checked behind me. They hadn't moved, they were silent, unfazed.

They were all the docile ones, those content to make do with water.

I could hear the constant dripping into pools and could make out a progression of figures sipping from it using cupped hands and reused bottles. So many of them, mesmerized by my light.

I could have cut myself open in that fall and they would have seen my blood as an offering—maybe that's how it started, how they turned from one kind of infected to the other: that first easy taste. I could become trapped—could end my life down here. These streets were ready to eat you alive. I shuddered; cold, the creepy someone-walking-over-your-grave kind of feeling.

A new noise: a shuffling, bumping, hum through the main pack, getting closer. There was movement among the masses, someone pushing and shoving their way forward. I wound the flashlight brighter, tried to see farther back behind me, the way out of here. Further commotion as someone pushed their way through the crowd, the Chasers nearest me parting aside.

A Chaser burst through, given a wide berth by the

others. He looked at me and wiped the back of his sleeve across his bloodied mouth.

I turned and ran.

I hit a turnstile at a full run and somersaulted over it, landing in a mess and struggling to get to my feet.

The Chaser clawed at the back of my bag, caught me.

I swung around and hit him with the bottom of my closed fist to the side of his head, and the way he'd held me and the surprise of my fight made him lose his footing and he was knocked to the ground.

I vaulted an overturned vending machine, almost at the glow of daylight that shone down the snowed-in stairs out of here.

The sound of my pursuer behind me, back in the chase.

I took to the stairwell as fast as I could, panting my way through the thigh-high snow drift. I looked back and he was there, five paces behind, and behind him—all those Chasers. Some watching, some not, so many eyes witnessing this hunt, so many haunted gazes about to see more brutality. My hand stung and I looked down at it. Red blood dripping freely onto white snow.

I was almost at the top, and my legs burned from the effort.

I looked up. Icy snow covered most of the exit, but there was a small hole leading out. I held my blood-ied fist out in front of me like a battering ram—a warm stream of fluid flowed through my knuckles as I clenched it.

I smashed through, almost tripped on the final step at street level and scrambled across the road.

The Chaser emerged. Those eyes. Only for me.

I ran for my life. Stumbling through the street grid-locked with smashed cars, sliding over a cab's bumper, the crash-bang of the Chaser shadowing me.

Around the corner, I turned immediately into the dark interior of a convenience store. I scanned my surroundings and rushed to a spot in the store where I could see the front door through the smashed windows. I slid down in the aisle and squatted on the floor, my head resting against a shelf, staring into middle-distance at the doorway, a bright rectangle of gray-white daylight.

A silhouette filled the space.

I inched backwards. Enclosed by darkness, my pulse chattered my teeth as I tried to calm my breathing.

He came into the store. Short and wiry, alert. Hunting.

I reached behind my back to the side pocket of my pack. Silent movements by me, the uneven rhythm of his gait as he treaded the aisles looking for me. The Glock pistol was in my hands and it shook—my whole body was shaking. My shoulders were tight, and I couldn't breathe properly.

I remembered holding this gun the first time. As my finger had slipped into the trigger guard, it'd felt both dangerous and comfortable. But part of me had wanted to be rid of it, to throw it away. Then I'd become more nervous as my target approached, as if I were invisible. I remembered pointing it at a boy, gaunt and tired, no less a victim and refugee than I was.

Now, I put the pistol into my coat pocket. I didn't want to shoot anyone, not now, never again. I stayed there and watched him for three seconds that dragged on like three hours. I had to move. I visually measured the number of strides to the front door, and ran for it.

The Chaser appeared at the end of the aisle in front of me—caught me by the backpack, dragged me right off my feet.

"No!" I yelled and reached into my pocket, swinging up my gun hand as his head bent down to mine—the heavy butt of the loaded pistol connected with the side of his head.

He fell on top of me—a dead weight—and lay there, motionless but for the tiny in-and-out motions of air as his chest rose and fell. He'd live, for now. I squirmed and wriggled my way out from under him.

When I left the store I clung close to the outside of the buildings, hugging one facade and then the next. That hole in the intersection was a dark mouth into hell, another reminder that this city could eat me alive at any second.

13

Rockefeller Plaza looked as I remembered it: the snow-covered fire engines, the massive crater where the ice rink used to be.

I walked around taking in the familiar surroundings, and seeking out someone undeniably real. A new piece to this puzzle that I was sure would somehow lead me home: Felicity.

I checked my watch: almost 11 A.M. If Felicity had shown when I'd said I would, then I was too late. The only movement now was the flapping of flags, the only thing I could feel was the cold of the wind cutting through my layers and whipping around the buildings.

There were some footprints in the snow. I followed them, lost in the pattern that led me across the street to the NBC News studio where they merged with other sets—large, haphazard in their direction. My ears pricked as a far-off explosion echoed around the buildings, but then it was gone as quickly as it had come.

As I stood just inside the entrance of 30 Rock I recognized the smell: so comforting, like coming home. All seemed as I'd left it. I thought about making a quick trip upstairs, to pack some gear, but the clothes and food and whatever else I'd stockpiled up there I could find anywhere, far closer to street level. But the thought of being high above this city, in a place I knew well, seemed so tempting. Just a quick look . . .

I took out my flashlight, wound the plastic handle for a minute and flicked it on. My hands shook with the prospect of what was ahead, a balanced mixture of excitement and fear. The LEDs were very bright, but did not penetrate far into the darkness of the lobby, nor spread out wide. The stark white-blue light sucked the life colors from everything that I scanned the beam over. Back in that subway station, it had turned those pale faces of the Chasers into something even more frightening, as if their skin were translucent, their eyes black beetles, their shadows darker than they ought to be.

I entered the gloom of the fire escape, the pistol in my other hand, and looked around. Two nights away from here and nothing seemed to have been disturbed. I shut the door behind me. The silence was so familiar. But this wasn't home. This was empty fear far outweighing any excitement.

I left the ink-black stairwell and sucked in the cold air of the bright winter's day around me. This shattered lobby wasn't comfortable. That journey upstairs in the pitch dark was no longer a choice for a better time. I backed out the door of the lobby and took in deep breaths, sinking to the cold paved ground. I couldn't go up those stairs again. I didn't want to know what I might find.

I remembered seeing an overturned postal truck on the block past 49th Street. It was still there, lying on its side, the mail that had spilled into the street from its rear doors long since covered with water, snow, and ash. I squatted down and shone my flashlight inside the truck—nothing, no living thing. I pulled out a couple of massive bags of mail, then tipped them out and folded the empty canvas bags into my backpack.

I headed back along 49th the way I'd come, trying to work out my next move. I could radiate out from here and search for signs of Felicity. I looked back to 30 Rock, looming large behind me, the low winter sun hitting its zenith to the south; it would be warm up there in that tower, behind the glass, in that sun.

"Which way?" I said out loud, shuffling through the snow and kicking an empty Coke can. "Which way do I go?"

Like I expected an answer. The mind draws conclusions from anything and everything, and I knew my own answer was what my gut was telling me: head south. Was that the pull of home? The lure of more sun in the day? Or did I need to head someplace else to get to where I really needed to go—check out places below Midtown I'd yet to see, look for easy routes off this island. But I resisted the call of the south—today I had to meet my promise, which was to bring food back to the zoo. Tomorrow was a different day.

★　★　★

I walked into a darkened grocery store, the way lit by my flashlight alone. The dim daylight filtering through the front windows only penetrated so far. There were a dozen or so mobile phones on the front counter, their boxes and packaging ripped open and scattered around the floor, like someone had been searching for something. I tried a few—some dead, some missing their batteries, one working and showing no network. The landline phone was smashed, its pieces on the floor. The cash register was open and empty but for small coins.

The first thing I did was to find some antiseptic and dressing, and some new gloves, and wash my newly cut hand by the light of the window, the wound not as bad as the bleeding suggested. I undid my pack, pulled out the two canvas postal bags and began to fill them with a mix of canned goods.

A shuffling noise, coming towards me, made me want to run. My flashlight wouldn't reach the entire length of the aisle. I wound the charge handle—the loudest thing I'd ever heard—and the beam grew brighter. I could just see—

A dog. A Labrador cross. His big sad eyes shone back at me, ears down, face friendly.

"Hey, boy . . ."

He didn't respond, just watched me.

I reached out to him and he growled, showing his teeth. He was lean but not skeletal; he'd been scavenging all these days. I looked through the shelves of tinned food, popped several cans of cat food and tipped them near him on the floor. He edged closer, wary, sniffing the air, his eyes never leaving mine as I backed away and left the store.

After a few blocks dragging the bags behind me, I found a well-stocked deli. Its windows were blown in, and snow had drifted inside the broken glass and through the open door, filling the front half of the shop. I made my way through it slowly, carefully, until it was just a dusting on the tiled floor. The display counters were all dry goods, grains, and pastas, along with jars of pickles and preserves.

I bagged coils of cured sausage and salami, some vacuum-packed portions that still looked good. The next fridge was overpowering in smell and contained cheeses—some wheels looked about as heavy as me. I collected as much as I could stuff into a bag.

I had so far packed supplies for the zoo's hungry mouths and plenty that was good for us. The other bag I filled with bagged and boxed grains and cereals, dried and tinned fruits, some staples. I added some containers of honey, long-life milk, and jars and cans of the odd delicacy—artichokes, olives, cheese, pickles; things I guessed Rachel might like. I looked forward to showing her all this food, taking my time to reveal it item by item, to share my spoils with someone, with another person like me.

This would show Rachel that I was trustworthy, that I was willing to support her and her quest. Question was, would she reciprocate?

I dragged the bags behind me. Each weighed easily forty pounds. I kept going like that for the rest of the block, then stopped, rested, arms on fire and hands aching. I sat on a cab's roof looking up and down the street. At this rate, it might take me until nightfall to get back to the zoo. Worse, the bags might spill their contents, damaged by all the scraping against raw as- phalt in the patchy snow, or from where they had snagged on sharp debris.

"New plan," I said out loud. "Try some cars."

Every one of them in the street that looked like it could get moving, I tried. None would start. Some ticked over, and a cab almost caught, only to have the battery die out at the penultimate crank of the starter- motor. I thought of Dad's old Ford in which he'd taught me to drive, how we had to push-start that sometimes. Maybe I could push one of these, but there was no room to pick up momentum, and with the snow and rubble on the road it was near impossi- ble to shift them beyond rocking back and forth on the spot. After half an hour I'd muscled a little Volks- wagen enough to roll two feet in the snow. I'd bagged all this food and I was stuck here, wasting time.

I needed a truck like the one driven by those army guys. Or maybe I could put something like a metal panel under the bags, something smooth-running if used like a sled, to pull the bags up to the zoo. Even if I had to take one at a time; one today and come back for the other one tomorrow. That could work.

I walked away from the stuffed mail bags towards some wrecked cars, scanning around for something to use.

"Stealing mail?" a man's voice asked.

14

He came and stood close to me, constantly looking north. He was about my age, dark unruly hair visible from the edges of his white winter cap, a head taller than me and broader across the shoulders, strong but lean.

"Yeah, that's exactly what I'm doing," I said, "stealing mail."

I saw the pump-action shotgun in his hands. He was staring intently, but not at me, his clear blue eyes framed by black-rimmed glasses, scanning Park Avenue. "Seriously, what you got in there, food?"

"What's it to you?"

He looked down at me for a second, and then back to the street, eyes darting around.

"If it's food, or something you need, I'll give you a hand," he said. "If it's money or gold or mail or some dude's used underwear, you're on your own."

Another survivor. I liked the way he talked: serious and funny at the same time, no wasting time with discussions of blame and anger. I sensed something softer beneath his stern exterior.

"I'm fine on my own," I said, lifting one bag and dumping it as far as I could reach, then repeating the process with the other. "And yeah, it's food. I'm not after some dude's drawers. Not that there's anything wrong with that."

"Nothing wrong with that?" he asked, looking at me, the start of a smile on his face.

"What are we talking about?" I hefted the bags another pace on up the road.

"Your perverted tendencies," he said, preoccupied, something changing in him as he looked up Park Avenue—a new stillness—then he ducked down, moved across the footpath in a crouched run and hid behind an overturned newspaper stand.

"Leave your stuff there," he whispered.

"What?"

"Just leave it," he said. "Get over here, quick!"

I rushed to his side, squatting down next to him.

"They're coming," he said. "Keep down. They're coming."

We kept low to the ground. I couldn't hear anything or anyone, certainly not like the arrival of yesterday's soldiers with their trucks. "They just rounded the corner up there."

"Who's 'they'?" I asked, sitting there on the ground looking up at him. Chasers? Soldiers? Other survivors?

"Them," he said, pointing.

I peered cautiously around the edge of the newspaper stand.

Down Park Avenue, appearing around the corner

from 53rd Street, were three Chasers. The deranged, hunt-you-down-for-what's-in-your-veins kind. It was so very easy to pick them from the other kind now: those who just drank whatever water they could find were now shells after thirteen days of no nutrients.

"This is what they do now," he whispered to me.

They moved with purpose, alert, on the hunt, blood on their chins and around their mouths, glistening as if they'd just had a fresh taste.

"I've seen them—"

"No, this is new. They're a scout team." He shifted position a little, readying for action, not taking his eyes off them. "Part of a bigger hunting party."

Watching the Chasers near, I pulled the Glock from my coat pocket and saw his eyes widen at the sight.

"You don't need that," he said. He motioned to his own gun, pulled a shell from his jacket pocket and passed it to me—a funny plastic cartridge the size of an asthma ventilator. "I got this from a cop station— it's a riot gun; shoots rubber bullets and little beanbags like that. It'll put them down for a bit, nonlethal."

I went to pass it back.

"You keep it," he said. "Souvenir."

"But if they come—"

"If they come close, even right up to us, we're not gonna go killing them," his look was full of disappointment or disgust. "These are people—they're sick, but they're Americans, yeah? You wanna do that? Kill?"

"No, but—"

"You wanna kill them, that's your show. I'll split and leave them to you."

He paused like he was actually giving me this opportunity to murder. Was it some kind of test? I'd set out, looking for people, for community, so maybe he was doing the same. Was I the kind of company he wanted to keep? I no longer knew who to trust—why wouldn't he be the same?

"No," I said, looking at the loaded gun in my hand, not for the first time wanting to give it away. "I don't want to kill them."

"Good," he replied, pumping a round in his shotgun. "I'll drop them, then we double around 52nd to Lexington, got it?"

"I've got to take that food with me."

"You're tripping, we gotta leave!"

"I have to—" I started to protest.

"We can't."

"Then count me out."

He looked at me, measured my resolve.

"Fine," he said. "One bag each."

I nodded.

"But if it comes to it," he said, "I'm not gonna get killed for a bag of food, so I'll ditch it—and you—if I have to."

"Okay."

"Okay. I'll count down, you make it to the bags and I'll drop these guys. We leave once the third is down. You'll follow me, got it? And put that pistol away before you shoot someone with it."

I pocketed the Glock and the beanbag shotgun cartridge.

With his gloved left hand, he counted down from

five, first his thumb, then a finger extending in time with each stride the Chasers took towards us.

"I'm Caleb," he said, matter-of-factly.

"Jesse."

His counting hand moved to the pump-action handle and he walked out to the street. The three Chasers looked up from the snow and saw him. I rushed over to the canvas bags.

Caleb took aim. They started running straight for us, while I began dragging the bags down Park Avenue. Caleb fired a shot—a Chaser collapsed. Oblivious to their fallen comrade the other two continued towards us, picking up pace with each stride, thirst in their eyes. Caleb loaded a new round and fired again, the boom deafening, another Chaser down. He pumped, reloaded and fired, but this time the Chaser slipped so the round was off-target. He pumped again—

Click.

"No way!" He pulled some rubber bullets from his coat pocket and started hurriedly feeding them into the breech of the shotgun.

The Chaser was on his feet again and sprinting from the mark.

"Hurry!" I yelled to Caleb, the Chaser seconds from him.

Caleb pumped to reload, aimed, and the Chaser was blown onto his back, yelling and writhing in pain.

The first shot Chaser was squirming, twisting on the ground, but looking like he was readying to get up, get back in the chase. The second was on his hands and knees, vomiting blood onto the street where he collapsed again. Caleb slung the shotgun's strap across his chest and took both canvas bags from me, hefting them clear off the ground. Then we ran.

15

I heard my heart beating inside my ears, and sucked hard at the cold air as we sprinted. One block, two, through a building's doors and out the other side onto another street, another block north.

Caleb stopped at the next corner, dropped the bags and doubled over, heaving.

"Put one of them over my shoulder," I said to him.

He nodded, too exhausted to voice a reply, and we were off.

"Hardly—done—exercise," he said, struggling to get air as we jogged, "since I hurt my knee in high school."

"What sport?" I asked, barely able to carry this one bag in the half a block we'd traveled.

"Basketball," he said. "I'm nothin' now—I used to have game."

"Mad skizzles, huh?"

"Not LeBron mad," he said of the NBA player, and we laughed through our exhaustion.

"What position?"

"Power forward," he replied, smiling at the memory. "They called me the Hebrew Hammer. If my knee had held up, I could've gone somewhere with it, but I decided to make college a place for learning instead of playing."

"Good plan."

"Yeah, right?" Caleb said. "Except looking around me now, I'm kinda thinking my planned undergrad in literature is a little misplaced. A stint in the Marines would have come in handy about now."

"Yeah, well, who'd ever predict this."

Caleb didn't respond. We crossed the street, weaving between the crashed cars, frozen in time from the moment of the attack.

"Do you have an idea where we're going?" I asked, looking over my shoulder. I couldn't see the Chasers, but I knew they weren't far behind, tracking us.

"57th and Park," he replied. It got darker like a switch had been thrown and soon it started snowing again.

"What's at 57th and Park?" I tried to remember the streets that had become familiar to me. There was no time to check my worn Manhattan map.

"My crib," he said. "It's safe."

Caleb's crib was a bookstore at the corner of Park Avenue and East 57th Street. The Ritz Tower rose above it; the bookshop had the bottom floors of retail space and I stood now, breathless, looking up. My dad would like this building. The three-story limestone base was finely detailed, the imposing tower itself set back at the fourth floor.

"Over here," Caleb said, pausing at a car. We stashed the bags of food in its unlocked trunk.

I couldn't see if the Chasers were after us and I didn't want to wait out in the open to find out. In the few blocks we'd traveled, Caleb had further convinced me with stories of these organized hunting groups, and I was keen to get inside.

"Setting traps?" I said. "Really?"

"Yesterday I saw some setting an ambush on one of the weaker ones."

"What kind of ambush?"

"They seemed to be herding him with coordinated attacks," he said as he fumbled with gloved hands with the keys to the bookstore, "from three different directions, before corralling him into a crater in the street. Then they stoned him until he lay still."

I pictured this image; it was as real as I ever wanted such a scene to be.

Behind us, on the opposite corner of the street, the Citibank building lay in burned-out ruins, a ghost from the past, the charred remains of a stack of hundred dollar bills blowing in the breeze. In the minute or so it took to open the store's doors, the snowfall became so heavy that I could no longer see across the street. I imagined those chasing us emerging from behind its veil, demons in my view, out of nowhere.

"I've seen them hunt, day and night," he said, holding the door open for me. I dashed through. "Another time, I watched them from a window, a pack of them, as they tracked and sneaked up on a wounded one."

"One of the other kind of infected?"

"They're culling them," he said, locking the door behind us. "Like wolves—killing rivals so that there's less pressure on the prey."

Caleb made them out to be hunters, more organized than I'd believed, and I was surprisingly grateful; I craved any information he could share, anything that would help.

Finally inside, with the outside shut out, I felt my heart rate settle. Our surroundings were just visible in the dim light; between the book stacks, the space was crammed with sports gear.

"This place safe?"

"Stores like this are more fortified than apartments," Caleb said, catching his breath after he locked the doors behind us and then dropping a metal bar into brackets across them; the barrier looked as though it would stop a battering ram. "Far safer from attack, see? Modern commercial spaces like this have toughened laminated glass." He rapped his knuckles on the door, emphasizing his point, then put down his small pack and shotgun, took off his boots, coat and hat. He was tall and rangy, leaner than I'd expected.

This was a good spot for me—safe, as Caleb said— and I was only two blocks from the Pulitzer Fountain at the corner of Central Park, and it was just a few blocks north from there to the zoo. I could drag those bags and be at Rachel's in an hour or so; less if I made a decent sled. Meanwhile, I could find out more about my enemy the Chasers—Caleb seemed to have been studying them closely. He also knew a lot more about the city than I did—more places to keep out of harm's way.

"I spray-painted all these windows black," he explained, "and left some eye-holes in each, covered with those pieces of black copy paper—so I can look out."

"Cool. Good idea." It wasn't pitch dark, though, with just enough daylight filtering through to see around inside while keeping prying eyes away. I rested against a counter, my breath almost back to normal, my clothes soaked through from our flight across the winter's ground.

"By the time those Chasers were back on their feet, we'd turned off the block and with the snow covering our tracks there's no way they'd know where we are now," I said to Caleb, trying to sound convinced by my own words.

There was a bang on the glass.

I froze, looked to Caleb. He rushed over to the far corner and peered out beneath the taped-up paper flap, jumping back at another bang on the window near him. Neither of us spoke or moved for a full minute, then he peered through the peephole again.

"They've gone," he said. There was a final bang farther away, and then it was quiet. "They went down the wrong street—and you're right, the snow would have covered our tracks by now."

I nodded.

"Take a load off, have a rest and catch your breath," Caleb said, as he climbed some stairs and disappeared into a room out the back.

I checked my watch. It was 1 P.M. Plenty of daylight left, if the snowstorm cleared. I'd stay an hour. Two, tops. See what he knew. See if he was planning to leave. He could be useful to us.

Already I was thinking of us as a group—me, Felicity, Rachel, and Caleb. None of them had met—it would be my job to bring them together. How hard could it be? Dave, Mini, Anna and I had had hardly anything in common, least of all our backgrounds. Dave and I hadn't really got on at the start of the camp, but we'd formed a bond by the time we made that final subway journey. Wouldn't it be so much easier to bond with the living, especially if everyone wanted the same thing? Escape. Survival. In whichever order we could manage. But could I assume we all wanted the same thing? Would I even find Felicity?

"Come up and grab a drink," Caleb said, hanging over the railing and showing some cans of soft drink. "Promise I don't bite."

I dumped my backpack and wet shoes by the sales counter, hung my coat over the end of a bookshelf and trudged upstairs. The next level up had a café where chairs and tables were scattered around; it felt good to be above street level with what would be, on a clear day, long views out over 57th and Park Avenue through the arched windows.

"Up here," he said, "show you my chill zone."

Caleb passed me a can of drink and I followed him up another flight of stairs to a smaller space with cur-

tained windows. I collapsed into a beanbag and settled in.

"This is the shiz, huh?" he said, cracking open his
Sprite.

He flicked a switch on a power-board, and the
room was lit by clear hoses of LED tube lighting,
jerry-rigged around the whole mezzanine. This level
was set up with all kinds of gear, a more extravagant
version of what I'd had at 30 Rock: two massive LCD
screens with game consoles, beanbags, couches, and
some big plastic tubs stuffed with packets of junk food.

"The only thing you're missing is a foosball table," I
said, popping my can and drinking fast.

"I tried; it was too heavy to get up here," he said,
slopping down into a beanbag and flicking on the TV
and Xbox. "Come have a crack at this, I've been waiting for someone's butt to kick."

We cranked out a few rounds of games, basketball
mainly, until I had to retire because my beat-up hands
were aching.

"Generator's good."

"Got a couple of them, just in case," Caleb said.
"Just run the one at a time in daylight hours when I'm
here, gas it up each night."

I told him about my set-up in 30 Rock—how I'd
dragged a generator all the way up sixty-five flights of
stairs. He laughed at that for a few minutes and then
passed over a couple of chocolate cookies from the
stash beside him. I told him about the soldiers.

"So they got into Manhattan via road?"

"Which means there's a way out," I said.

"Somewhere up north . . ." Caleb said, thoughtfully, plowing through a row of Oreos dipped in coffee. "If they had a couple of trucks as big as you say, means they could use them as muscle."

"Exactly!" I said. "They drove in, pushing their way clear—they must have cleared a path. A path we could use."

"We?"

"Yeah, you know, to get out of here."

He paused, thinking about it. "And get through these roadblocks how?"

"They got through."

"Armed dudes, maybe they were National Guard or something official," he said. "I don't think it'd be that easy, for me or you or whoever."

I nodded, and said as convincingly as I could: "Bet there's people congregated up there. Whole towns and cities unaffected."

"For sure or maybe?"

I hesitated. "Maybe."

"Maybe," he said, picking absently at the top of a can of drink. "Look, yeah, there's likely places unaffected even if all the major cities have been hit. There might be quarantine stations and stuff at roadblocks or checkpoints. But those guys you saw—it seems weird it was so few soldiers."

"I know."

"Could be they came to steal gold or something. That's what always happens in times like this."

"Looting?"

"Wars, disasters, whatever—soon as there's no law and order there's always opportunists." Caleb looked up at me. "And how about how one of them told you to head to where it's *colder*... I guess that makes sense, but it was weird that he would give you that info, if he was here just lootin' or whatever."

"What do you mean 'makes sense'? That it's worse in a warmer climate?"

"Yeah, I mean, if this was an aerosol weapon, in the air, heat makes stuff like that more effective," he said and nodded, as though he was thinking about it. "Or was he saying the *effects* are worse? Like the differences in the infected? Like if only a small percentage here are deranged hunters, maybe there's a greater proportion of them like that where it's warmer and the infection makes them more screwed up?" He smiled. "Hungry?"

"Yeah," I said. "Starving."

Caleb got up and I yawned, stretched, and looked out the window; it was almost pitch black outside. I checked my watch: 4:45. My stomach turned. I couldn't believe how easily I'd lost time like that; so carefree, so selfishly easy. I'd told Rachel I'd be back later today. I'd promised her, as her workmates had done when they'd left.

"Look, I really should get that food delivered . . ." I said, not even convincing myself.

"To who? Your friends need it tonight?"

"Well, not exactly . . ." I told him about Rachel, how most of that food was for the animals and how they were still good for a while.

"She's survived on her own this long, what's another night?"

"It's just—I promised her I'd be back."

"She'll understand. It's a mad world out there, right? No point in risking life and limb just to keep a promise."

The way he said it, I felt almost stupid for bringing it up in the first place.

"Yeah, I know."

"Look, you might as well just stay here the night," he said. "I can help you deliver those bags in the morning, if you like? Safer that way. No sense you getting killed for food when it's not exactly a case of life and death. Right?"

I nodded, still not sure what to do. It didn't make sense to trudge all the way to the zoo in the dark. More risk than it was worth. I'd stayed alive so far because I'd been careful. I should stay that way.

And this *was* a sweet setup. This, I thought, entering the café's kitchen—this was temptation. This was, as Caleb said, *the shiz*.

16

We sat at a table, a feast before us. We'd grilled some beef patties, made well-stacked cheese burgers, and I added sliced beetroot and a fried egg. I picked up the hot, dripping burger. I took a bite, savoring it, then thought of Rachel.

What was she eating? Was she okay? Here we were, eating in the café while she was back there alone. The hum of the generator was comforting and accusing.

There was no silence with Caleb, no weary night filled with quiet company. We talked about things I'd talk about with friends back home—sport, movies, games, girls. All of it so normal, transportational even: like I was back home and staying the night at a mate's place. I realized he was a Peter Pan–like character, residing in fun, using it as a coping mechanism; deep denial, hidden by fun and games. It was easy company to reside in.

"So, why a bookshop?" I asked. "Why hole up here?"

"I work here," he replied. "Took a year out before starting school at Columbia—an expensive education, and so here I am in Midtown, selling books to people in suits and heels. Means I'm free of my folks, can afford to live with friends, all that."

"Seems a sweet gig to me."

"Yeah, it is," he said with a little laugh. "Least I like it. It's easy, you know? My mom's a bit bummed out by it, and Dad hates that I still do it—he works in publishing."

"Editor?"

"Was. Sales now."

"So he sells books too?"

"Yeah, I guess," Caleb said, laughing. "But he's like a global director for a company that owns the publishing company and other stuff—defense and aerospace industries, paint and carpet factories, the usual evil conglomerate. He spends most of his time synergizing 'backwards overflow' or something."

"Sounds un-American."

"I know, right?" he said. "Sad thing is, that's where we've got to. There and beyond."

Did he mean now, after this attack, or before?

"Why doesn't he like you doing this?"

"My dad? Thinks I could do better or that I'll get sucked into working here forever instead of going to college," he said. "Mom, too, but she won't say it. He always says things like that, while Mom's busy trying to set me up with so and so's fugly daughter, so I hardly ever go home for dinner even though they're not twenty minutes' walk from where I live . . . You know, this past year I spoke more often to my mom on Facebook than in person. Weird, huh?"

"Seems okay," I said. I liked that he spoke about

them in the present tense. "So you were stuck at home until you finished school or whatever, and since then you've just needed some space, yeah?"

He shook his head. "I boarded high school. Same as my dad, his dad, his dad . . ."

"Right."

Up close, across the table and in this light, I could see he had baggy dark rings under his eyes as though he hadn't slept well in ages. He seemed like he would have been quiet in his normal life, before all this, probably a pretty isolated guy. He had that kind of look about him. Maybe, in some selfish way, this was some kind of blessing for him, a chance to break the cycle, if only his character would let him.

But what did I know? Maybe he wasn't like that at all. Maybe he had been an out-there party guy, a family guy, anything *but* a loner, and that was just what he'd been forced to become.

"So, Aussie Jesse, you like New York?"

"Sure. I mean, I liked it a lot more before all this happened though."

He laughed. "Ha. But the *people*; they're so self-centered a lot of the time. Keep to themselves. Don't get involved."

"I hadn't really got that," I said. I tried to remember seeing any of that kind of behavior, but everyone I'd met before the attack had been so kind, so helpful, so happy to meet me.

"You haven't seen it because you weren't here long enough," he said. "And because Americans love Aussies."

"We have followed you into every war you started."

"Yeah, thanks," he said. "But seriously, I mean, don't get me wrong, New York's the bomb. I'd rather live here than any other city; we got it all and then some. It's just—take where I live, for instance, just a stop out of Manhattan, on the other side of the East River. It's like we're another country away. Doesn't have that neighborhood feel anymore; before this, I mean."

Division. Friction. A vision seared into my consciousness. "Funny how the world turns, hey?"

"Yeah, it is." He looked at his plate, a million-mile stare that suggested maybe the now was indeed affecting him too. He reached for an orange plastic prescription bottle, found the one he was looking for among the few on the table, then shook a couple little white pills loose and swallowed them.

"For my knee," Caleb explained. He looked around the room with what may have been either pride or nostalgia. "I like working here. It's easy, I get to hang with people I like, and I don't take work home except for advance reading copies of books. I just didn't want to go straight into more study, especially since I've got no idea what I want to do. I mean . . . I was thinking of traveling, but now?"

I looked around, the shadows of the book stacks disappearing into darkness. "This job here sounds good—I like reading. Quite a few comics. And I just got a copy of *Siddhartha*."

Anna's book. I remembered her talking about it. I could picture the note she'd inserted for me—something about its being her dad's favorite. I could see her careful handwriting. But where was the book now? Had she actually given it to me? *Pride and Prejudice* was another one of hers. When I got home, I'd find a copy. Think of her as I read it.

"That's a pretty neat novel," Caleb said. "Reading, I could do it all day, but I also like writing, when I've got the inspiration."

"What kind of writing?"

"Been working on a comic series; might end up being a graphic novel."

"About?"

"It's a work in progress, but my characters all have heightened natural abilities—kinda tapping into using more of their brains, a higher-evolved type scenario. Most of the stuff on the shelves in here is all soap opera and melodrama in place of a good story that's well-told. Anyway, my thing's a long way off, and meantime I have to pay the bills."

"Not anymore, hey," I said, regretting it immediately. What was outside, what was beneath the surface of every line of our conversation, hidden in every minute I'd been here, was what he was shutting off from the outside world. There he was, trying to sound upbeat about it, to have a career in this world. Didn't he see those desolate streets like I did? Did he think everything would go back to how it was?

"Thought I might just start my own company for my writing, release it all electronically, for iPads and stuff. What about you?"

"What do I want to do?" I bounced my balled napkin off the wall and Caleb caught it. I was going to say, *Does it matter anymore?* but I knew it did—around Caleb, it actually *felt* like it did, like there'd be a tomorrow that would bring us back to how things were. With him, there was a sense of possibility, more than bleak denial. "Two years ago, I thought about joining the Air Force, becoming a fighter pilot, maybe even going from there into politics."

"But now?"

"I don't know. I guess now I've seen this . . ." I swept my hand around, gesturing outside. "I don't know. I want to contribute, I know that. I just don't know what *now* is . . ."

Caleb nodded, silent while we watched the candle burn between us.

"I just want to make something," Caleb said quietly. "Make something that lasts, you know? Some kind of art that makes people think, raises more questions than it answers."

Conversation with Caleb was so normal that it was surreal. I mean, I liked art and stories as much as the next person, but didn't we need more than that right now? It was clear to me we'd sat here for long enough. We'd talked to that point where it could get into uncomfortable territory, like I'd felt often enough in those first twelve days. If Caleb had a black dog of depression and despair lingering in the shadows of his otherwise Peter Pan–like psyche, I didn't want to know about it. Couldn't I have one friend who didn't need me to give anything? Couldn't there be one who I could take *from,* an escape from reality?

17

"**N**o!" I screamed, sitting up with a start. Caleb was looking down at me. He had shaken me awake.

"You okay?" he said.

I nodded and he walked away.

I was wet with sweat, hot, could see it was light outside.

"What time is it?" I called out.

"Just after ten," he hollered back.

"What?!" I found my watch on the floor. Almost eleven. I was too late for Felicity. Again.

Shit.

Even if she were alive, even if she'd found my note and bothered turning up when I said I was going to, after two no-shows, she'd not bother turning up again, would she?

I lay back, holding my head in my hands. I drifted from my disappointment in myself for oversleeping to thinking about the nightmare. I tried to shut out the visions but they remained fresh and vivid. Caleb was in it, the girls too—both Rachel and Felicity. We were running, but not from Chasers. We were up the top of Manhattan somewhere, up north, trying to get out, and soldiers were following us, hunting us; four of them, on horseback.

I sat up, caught my breath and calmed my heart rate. I got dressed fast.

I found Caleb upstairs on the terrace. He stood on the roof of the bookstore, glassing the city with powerful binoculars. The day was clear and the sun was nearing its lonely peak.

"You seen *Dawn of the Dead*?" he asked me.

I watched him, thinking about the way he made jokes whenever he could, because the alternative was—what—to be scared out of his wits? "The zombie movie?"

"Yeah," Caleb said, looking down at a group of docile Chasers drinking from a large flooded crater on Park Avenue. "Remember that scene when they're on the roof in the mall? There's that gun-shop owner across the parking lot?"

"Yeah," I said and laughed. "They picked out lookalikes in the crowd."

"And the gun store dude sniped them off—pop!" Caleb laughed. "Check out down there."

He pointed, passed the binoculars, and I tried my best to zoom in on the spot.

"Bill Clinton."

"No way!" I said. It may well have been him. "Looks a bit skinny, though."

"Couple of weeks of this liquids-only diet will do that."

"Next to him; blue jacket." I passed the binoculars over.

"Yeah?" he replied, scanning left. "Ha, no way!"

"Way," I said. "That's Lady Gaga."

"Good eye." He put down the glasses, took a big breath, looked around at what was left of his town. There were a couple of fires burning to the north, Harlem maybe, tall plumes of black smoke twisting into the air. "You look at this too much, gets you angry."

"Who do you think did this?" I asked.

"If I had to guess . . ." Caleb said, scratching his chin, "I'd say it probably had something to do with the DHARMA Initiative."

"Okay . . ." I laughed, remembering it from one of my favorite American TV shows. "So, what, we're gonna realize we're all dead in the finale?"

As soon as I said the words I felt sick. But Caleb only saw it as a joke.

"Yeah, something lame like that," he replied. "What I do know is that if this infection were a zombie plague, it would be classified as a Class Four outbreak."

"A what?"

"Doomsday event—the worst kind of outbreak."

"And you know that because . . ."

"Look around."

"I mean, you know the classification number?"

"Read it in a book about surviving zombie attacks."

"I don't want to know," I said as we went indoors. "Seriously, I've done all right so far, all alone, so to start reading fictional survival guides . . ."

"It's actually been pretty useful," Caleb said as he led the way downstairs. "You know, stories of zombies came from Voodoo. A bunch of stuff happened in Haiti way back in the day—"

"But these aren't zombies."

"Zombie-vampire hybrids, whatever. This is some kind of killer virus, though," he said as we descended the stairs into the bookstore. He scanned around with his beanbag shotgun, listened until he was satisfied the coast was clear. "And they might as well be un-dead. But anyway, there's even this book written by a Harvard professor—yeah, one of those smug crimson guys—who went to Haiti and studied the toxins they used to transform people—"

"I really don't want to know," I said. "Listen, Caleb, that food down there—I've got to get it to Rach."

"In the park?"

I nodded.

"With the thousands of infected hanging around the ponds and whatnot."

"It's where Rachel is."

"And you've got to deliver that food."

"Yep."

"Come on, then," Caleb said, getting his snow gear on. "I'll walk you to the corner of the park. Don't want you getting attacked outside my place so I gotta see your sorry ass all frozen there until some rat king carries you off."

18

I descended the stone stairs to the zoo, dragging one bag at a time down the slippery surface. Caleb had walked me to the corner of the park as he'd promised and then disappeared. He'd said he'd not been to the zoo since his parents took him when he was a kid. He'd trailed off and looked longingly to the northeast, turned, and walked away.

Maybe he didn't want to meet Rachel. That'd have to change fast if I stood any chance of getting the pair of them to try leaving Manhattan with me.

If he wanted space, I understood that: we all still needed our space, however lonely we'd become. In just two nights I'd grown used to that concept. At home it had always been that way for me; I was an only child who had moved around a bit, changing school a few times, and had always somehow adapted, always found my own center. I learned I could survive anywhere, that I'd be accepted as myself wherever we landed. I saw that possibility in New York, as though we all belonged there, wherever we were from, but didn't get the time to live it that way.

Looking up at the Arsenal's front doors my world changed again: the glass in the doors was broken, there was blood on the doorframes, blood down the hand-rail.

At the top of the stairs I shook the doors—they were still locked shut. That was a good sign. The break-in had cracked every pane of the laminated glass and there was a hole big enough to put my head through, dried blood coating the shards and staining the snow at my feet. I knocked hard on the brass frame, waited and listened, knocked again. All was quiet. I looked through the glass, cupping my hands against my face as I had done before. It was dark in there, I could see no movement.

"Rachel!" I called, as loudly as I dared.

My voice echoed inside the building and rattled around. Still no answer. I looked up to street level. Nothing sinister. The tiny thought at the back of my brain crept forward and developed into: maybe I should leave, go back to Caleb, forget about this place? I didn't want to find Rachel gone or worse . . . I paced the courtyard. The building, the street, the trees around me, everything was bare and barren. I heard the bark or yelp of an animal, a sea lion maybe. I had to see, I had to know.

I climbed a side fence, repeating my entry of the zoo from the other day. Everything seemed the same, although there had been a fresh coat of snow over-night. I scanned it for footprints. Nothing. That was good. I hoped that was good. The back doors were locked. That was definitely good.

I looked around the grounds, did a lap around the central pool, then ran over to the cafeteria.

"Rachel!" I called again. Into the cafeteria. Empty. The Zoo shop—more locked doors. "Ra—"

Rachel emerged from an equipment room. She looked spooked and stayed where she was; I ran over to her.

"I'm sorry I didn't come sooner. I met this guy, Caleb—"

"Are they still out there?"

"The Chasers? No, I didn't see anyone," I said, talking fast. "I meant to come straight back, but he's a good guy and we're all about the same age, and I was thinking how we'd be so much better off as a group. You know, safer."

She stood there, silent.

"Rachel?" Maybe it was too soon to mention the plan that was forming in my mind. Maybe I had more to do to earn her trust.

"You're sure they're not still there?"

"There're no Chasers. Rachel, I'm sorry I took so long. Are you okay?"

She replied with a half-nod. "Were you followed?"

"Just now? No."

"You're sure?"

"Yes," I replied. She looked like she'd been awake all night; my guilt amplified. "Why, what happened?"

"They came back."

"Came back?"

"The ones that followed you here the first time."

"You're sure it was them?"

"I saw them," she said. Her body and face looked tense, her eyes taking in every detail.

She looked so scared that I promised myself that I'd be there for her from now on, that I'd be more reliable. She might not be as fun as Caleb, but she needed me around. Sure, I'd come back with food before she'd run out, but I could see what mattered to her more was my being there, my keeping my word. If I had to do another food trip, I'd be better at it next time. And right now I'd prepare this place better, for her.

"The front doors are still locked," I said.

"They smashed at the glass with a steel pipe," she said. "I watched them beating on it until it started to break through, then I ran out here."

She looked back into the room. There was a little burner set up with a pot of water. In the dim light from the equipment room behind her there was a stack of blankets where she must have slept, or at least sat, listening.

"Can you make tea?" I asked, wanting to distract her. She nodded, and I could see her slipping into nurturing mode, her comfort zone. "I brought food, I'll go get it."

"Wait!"

"They're not there at the moment," I said, "but I'll have another look around, okay?"

She softened just a little more. "Okay."

"Can I have the key to the gate?"

Rachel took her keys from the lanyard around her neck and placed it over mine. She went inside while I ran back around to the front of the arsenal building to get the food. As I picked up the canvas bag I looked at the snow.

Footprints.

My heart skipped a beat before I realized that they were mine, only mine. I did a quick scan of the street, searching for any sign—nothing. Wherever they were, they'd gone before this last snowfall.

I dragged the bag down from Fifth, and took it through the gate with the other.

Rachel was busy at her work, as if with my presence and news she'd now hit reset; this was how I'd found her two days ago. I presented her with the food, and she came over and put her gloved hand on my shoulder, then pulled me in for a hug.

"Thank you for coming back," Rachel said, holding me. "I was worried. I was worried I'd never see you again."

Rachel was so small in my embrace. So fragile, a bird.

"I can look after myself."

I felt her warm tears running down my neck. She let go and sniffed into her sleeve, looked about her, blinking.

"I know you can," she said, watching her animals eat. "It's just . . . I thought maybe you'd not come back . . ."

"What, you thought I could just forget about you?" I said.

Sure, I had hopes and desires to get home and find it as I remembered it, but right now, Rachel and her tribe of animals felt like all I had. Caleb was his own guy. Probably needed me around less than we needed him.

"I could feel useful here," I continued, "if you'll let me help out more?"

She nodded and I followed her on her errands. I took the heavy work and it felt good. She told me about the animals and their needs and I asked about their habits and personalities and I could see clearly why this meant so much to her.

This was where I felt like my life had a purpose. This here, somehow, was where I felt closest to being home. As long as I was in this city, this was where I wanted to be. Until I could make it home, I would do what I could to help her.

19

Rachel worked at a pace that had me aching all over by sunset. We'd fed every animal, laughed a few times at the antics of the sea lions, and I'd spent a couple of hours clearing away some snow. All the food from the canvas bags was stashed away, and I had a good bearing now on what it would take to feed all these animals over the coming days. Beyond that . . . well, I didn't really want to think about that, least not today. I could see how easy it was for Rachel to take it a day at a time in this place and have whatever's going on outside these walls seem as distant as another universe.

"Yesterday, you got to Rockefeller Plaza on time?"

"Yeah," I replied, thinking of sleeping in this morning. "There was no sign she'd been there."

"You may have just missed her."

"Yeah, maybe." We collected some firewood from a stack in a storeroom. "Or she hasn't gone back home since I'd been there."

"To find your note."

"Yeah—because she would have showed, right?"

"I suppose. Unless she's come across a refuge or shelter of other survivors?"

"Yeah, I hope so."

"You're going to check again tomorrow morning?"

"I have to."

"Do you?"

Rachel could see in my look that, yeah, I had to.

Every time I passed a fence or a gate I looked out, expecting to see those Chasers reappear. It was only a matter of time. Rachel noticed me.

"They know we're here," she said. "They're out there, watching, waiting."

I could feel it, but I didn't want to let my fear of them show. I'd faced them before, up close, and come out alive. I'd do it again for her.

"They're probably just waiting for night to fall," she continued. "Or waiting for you to leave on another food trip."

"Then I should test that—head out, soon, see if they follow me." She looked at me like I was crazy. "That way, I'd know how many of them there are, maybe even see where they came from, how long it took them to make a move on me."

"That's crazy."

"I can outrun them."

"Accidents happen—you might slip or fall and then what?"

I thought back to falling through the road yesterday.

"Don't take them on if you don't have to. Don't encourage their behavior," she said. "Like any predators, they'll wise up fast to ways of getting what they need."

I just wanted to be better prepared, to understand them more. With that knowledge, when the day came for Rachel to leave with me—for she surely had to leave one day—we'd stand a better chance.

"They're close by," she said, "even if there's no sign of them right now: Central Park is their smorgasbord, where the bulk of other infected are congregated en masse, around the ponds and lakes. You said so yourself."

She was right. They were all around us, just out of view, never far away. Rachel hadn't stopped working all day, and had sweat on her face.

"Let's make dinner."

"I've got another fifteen minutes out here," she said, judging the light left before night set in.

"I'll make it."

"Sure," Rachel said, pausing to drink from her water bottle. "That'd be nice."

"Any requests?"

She shook her head. "Surprise me."

I entered the arsenal building with a spring in my step—I really wanted to do this, to thank her by cooking her a meal. This much was achievable for me: caring for one. But how she managed to do all that out there on her own—that was more than impressive.

Sometimes I wondered about my real mom, whether she had started up a new family, if she was caring for kids. Rachel was just a couple years older than me and was the greatest caregiver I'd ever seen. She deserved to not only get out of all this, but to be rewarded. How, I had no idea.

Inside was quiet, cold, eerie. I walked slowly along the carpet runner leading to the front door. I stopped behind a partition, peering around at the front doors. The wind whistled in through the broken glass. I needed to fix that, barricade those doors. I'd do it to-morrow.

Then I stopped.

No. No more tomorrows. I would not put things off anymore. Put them off into days that might not be there. As long as Rachel was here, I'd do my best to keep her safe.

I emptied a tall bookcase, dragged it to position up against the doors, restacked it, then added a desk, a few armchairs, and plenty of books and boxes of files from a front office. All up, there must have been a few hundred pounds stacked on and against that bookcase, itself a barricade against the glass. At the very least, it would slow down intruders long enough for us to hear them and make a break for it. I felt better for the construction, and headed upstairs with my backpack and a more comfortable feeling that I would not have someone creeping up behind me.

It took a few minutes of blowing against the embers to get the kindling to light, by which time I was out of breath and had filled the room with smoke, but it felt satisfying to have ignited the flames without splashing lighter fuel over the wood. The fire warmed and crackled, and soon small split logs became coals hot enough for cooking. The smell of the burning wood was different to that back home, but the memories came anyway—sitting around a campfire, my father there telling me stories—and I was happy for them to keep me company. You could get lost in memories like that.

Caleb had told me a recipe that would suit the ingredients I had. He'd given me some white wine, and I'd put half a bottle into the dish, along with chicken, rice, tinned tomatoes, and slices of onions, orange, garlic, some herbs and seasoning. Caleb had sworn by the chicken—it was from one of many tubs he had stashed on the snow-covered terrace. I had the pot slow-cooking on the side of the coals, it'd take about an hour and a half.

I stood at the window and watched Rachel down in the zoo grounds, hurrying to beat the darkness. For a brief moment I glimpsed the absolute truth of her world, and some reality of mine: she felt she belonged here, but we were both visitors. How long could she look after all these animals and not look after herself? I'd been here for just hours and I could see that all the work to be done was more than she and I could sustain. What would happen when food and water in the vicinity ran out? This was a no-win situation: we were living on stolen time.

Rachel came upstairs when it was dark out, moving so silently she startled me.

"Sorry."

"No, that's fine, just lost another year from my life."

Rachel laughed.

"It's so damn easy to get spooked in this city, I'm

probably running out of years to lose." I stoked the fire with another small split log. It spat and burned and smoked. The lidded pot sat heavy, almost ready. I glanced over at her as she took off her jacket and boots. "You know that feeling when you're alone, but it feels like there's someone around you?"

"I think so," Rachel said, motioning out of the window before drawing the thick curtains. "I feel like I'm being watched when I'm out there, out in the zoo grounds."

"I sense that too." That feeling of being watched—whether by Chasers or other survivors—was constant, but that was not what I had meant, not totally. I stirred the pot and put the lid back on.

"And I don't mean by those infected," Rachel added, taking her jumper off.

"Yeah, me either," I said, smiling. "I mean by those I miss."

She nodded and sat next to me by the fire. "Who do you think about?"

"A few people. My grandmother, she used to talk to my grandfather's ashes," I said, smiling at the memory buried somewhere in the brilliant hot embers before me. "Even though he was nothing more than ashes in an urn, she'd go about it like it was the most natural thing in the world—like he was right there in the room, listening, as she went about her day, talking to him."

"Well, he was there, wasn't he?"

"Yeah. He was . . . It was the only time I saw her truly happy, on her own, speaking to her dead husband." I smiled. "That, and when she'd hug me when I went to spend school holidays with her. Speaking to the dead and hugging me."

Talking to the dead had kept me alive.

"You had that too, didn't you?" she shifted over to the edge of her bed and rubbed her bare feet.

I nodded.

"With your friends from the subway here in New York?"

"Yeah."

"Then you know what it's like when you lose a friend or someone in your family and it's like they didn't really go," Rachel said, kneeling next to me and warming her bare hands by the fire. "Me too. My best friend died in a car accident when we were in seventh grade. I felt she was with me all through school and every day since. Not a day goes by when I don't think of her, when I don't hear her voice."

"Yeah?"

She nodded.

"You're lucky to have that," I said. "You're lucky she's always there."

"I'm just glad it's something I carry around in me," she said. "It doesn't have to be an urn on the mantel-piece. It doesn't wear out, get lost, depend on the up-keep like my work out there every day."

I watched her, her features in the warm light.

"The animals, me; we all eat, we all sleep, and we all leave, eventually."

I had a feeling she wasn't talking about the present.

"I had a boyfriend back home," she said. "We kept

it going for over a year; he'd come here or I'd head west, a few days here and there . . ."

"Too much distance?"

"Something like that. Still friends, just didn't quite work out."

She seemed happy to talk about it, and it was nice to hear this side of her.

"No one now?"

"New York's outta good guys," she said.

"If it wasn't before, it sure is now," I said. "I don't mean to make you more depressed about the reality of this situation, but if there was anything that these events have done, it's thin out the dating pool even further."

It took a moment for her to laugh, but when she did she was lost in it to the point of tears.

By the time Rachel had come back from the bathroom all cleaned up and changed into pajamas, I'd set two spots at the desk, with chairs and cutlery and napkins and some candles. The fire was restoked and the room was warm. I poured wine for her and served up, as Rachel sat opposite, looking down at her plate then up to me. She was the big sister I'd never had, and I loved making her this meal.

"This smells great," Rachel said.

"Thanks, I hope it tastes good." I told her the recipe was Caleb's, which gave me the chance to explain a bit about him.

"Tell me about your friends," she said over her glass of wine.

Why not? So I told her. I told her everything about Anna, Mini, and Dave. Explained all that I'd done to get me through those first days. This was my story, and I was getting good at telling stories, never embellishing, describing events as I saw them, reporting the truth as I knew it. I enjoyed passing on details, and there was one thing above all that I'd noticed in this new earth: when people listened to you, they listened to your every word, hung onto them, savoring information. We were all hungry for it—I couldn't imagine all the knowledge we were losing without information. It was somewhere, as long as there were people willing to listen, and talk and write. Even when I got home, I'd make sure I took this sense of observation and discourse with me. We needed to talk more, to listen more, all of us.

"We dressed up, pigged out on junk food, danced around to music, it was great," I said. "If I hadn't laughed so much with them, I'd have gone nuts. We spent a whole afternoon launching rotten food off the top of the building, joking that seventy stories below the apples and cabbages would pick up such speed that they'd blast right through parked car's roofs."

I laughed at the memory, so much that I had tears in my eyes and Rachel's face was lit up with laughs too.

"We'd laugh at the stupidest things," I said. Rachel listened and never seemed to think my story strange or judge me, just ate her food and laughed with me. It was great to talk like that, with no barriers, to share.

"I think you were lucky, Jesse. You did good."

"Yeah," I said. "Thanks. And thanks for listening—feels good to share it, with you."

She smiled. It was a smile that I hadn't yet seen; it radiated, like a great sentence or a good piece of music, so recognizably special that it could transcend the moment. Rachel may not be someone I could laugh with at stupid little things, not like Caleb, but I could tell her anything. Anything important, anything big. Like what I wanted to do. What we had to do. I painted a picture of truth that I felt would help persuade Rachel to move out from here.

"Can you imagine going home?"

My question bobbed in the water for a while, a float on a lure.

"Jesse, the day I most look forward to right now is when the tourists flock back to Times Square, the city is healthy again, and this nightmare is over."

Sleep came easily here, easier than back at 30 Rock, Felicity's apartment, or Caleb's. The room was cozy and warm, and this big old building felt like a fortress. We were right in the park—the place I'd come to associate the most with Chasers, with fear—yet I felt unbelievably safe and comfortable.

It was my second night here and I was being pulled into sleep. I needed to find Felicity, find a way to escape, to go home. But darkness was drawing, taking my conscious thoughts away.

It was a dangerous feeling.

20

"Huh?" Something had woken me. The fire glowed and crackled. Rachel was a still form under her quilts. The fire sparked again, its coals shifting. The log still had a few good hours of burning ahead, which meant it must only have been an hour or so since I'd nodded off.

I'd been entering that nightmare again, the soldiers on horseback, and to be away from it now, to be awake, was a relief; I was able to bear the reality. I should remember this scene—the crackling fire, Rachel peaceful in sleep—and this moment, for it was full of possibility, full of happiness. I watched the fire until I felt my eyes closing. A noise jolted me from my semi-lucid state. From downstairs?

The hallway.

I opened my eyes wide, my heart racing, my breath short. It was a tapping or a rattling, faint; there and then gone again. Just the wind seeping into the old building? Then silence . . .

I was alert, on edge, but overwhelmed with exhaustion and soon felt myself start to drift off, my body heavy. I rolled onto my back, looked up at the ceiling. *Stay awake.* The whitewashed timber paneling, the knots and grains forming patterns and shapes. *Stay awake.* I picked out a car, a mountain range, a fox, a face.

A louder bang. I sat up, wide awake now.

"Rachel?" I whispered. I looked across the room at her sleeping form. She didn't move. "Rachel?"

I got up fast, pulled on my jeans and coat and went over to Rachel; she was sound asleep, breathing slowly and rhythmically and smiling against her pillow. I reached for her shoulder but stopped: *let her be.* Part of me thought that if this was it, I should let her go like that. Most of me wanted to prove something.

I put on my shoes, pulling the Glock pistol from my FDNY coat pocket, making sure a round was loaded and ready to fire, and took a battery-powered flashlight from the bookcase.

My hand rested on the brass doorknob. Just a moment. I took a deep breath, then turned the handle, inched the door open, felt the cold air flood in.

The hallway was dark, quiet. I closed the door behind me, the faint glow of the fire just visible beneath it. We needed locks on these doors. What if someone got inside the building? It was quiet, not a sound or creak. Had I imagined those noises?

I shone the light ahead of me, down towards the stairs, to the left and into the bathroom. Nothing untoward.

I inched my way forward, the floorboards creaking under my weight. I reached the far end of the hall, where the noise had come from. The bright shaft of the flashlight beam illuminated the shadows. How I wished for a light switch; power and the security that came with it, freedom from the unknown, freedom from the surprises. The bathroom was empty, unchanged, silent, the buckets of water still lined up, just as they had been earlier. I went back out to the hall; so long, so dark, hoping the beam of bright light would scare away more than just the shadows.

The door opposite the bathroom was a little different from the others, the bottom corner black and charred, leaving a gap that let through a constant draught.

I watched that door, hesitating before opening it, not wanting to be reminded of another closed door back at 30 Rock—some doors should not be opened. I resolved that I had to check it for Rachel's sake. Inside, I found myself in some kind of lounge or reception room, burned out by fire some time ago; from the attack, I supposed, though Rachel had said nothing of it. Black soot surrounded the hearth and spread out along the floor before it and the timber wall paneling surrounding the door was blackened too, as if the flames had spewed forth to consume the room.

Why have I never opened this door before?

I felt as though I'd seen this image before, in the charred corpses at a road tunnel. There was a hole in the floor where it had burned clean through, a blackened beam and the topside of a plaster ceiling just visible below; a desk by a window with a burned-out antique globe, another skeleton of what had once been whole. It was so cold in here, spookily so, and quiet. I left, shutting the door behind me.

At the top of the stairs I waited and listened, a hand on the banister to steady myself. Maybe it had been the wind or an animal outside in the zoo? Maybe I had imagined it? I turned off the flashlight and sank down on the top step and sat there. So dark and so quiet. If I heard someone come up these creaky stairs I'd flick on the flashlight and blind them as they turned at the landing, shoot if I had to. What if there was more than one? I glanced back at the glow under the door to the room where Rachel was sleeping. I waited in silence and darkness.

Rustling. Another rattle-bang from downstairs.

Then behind me.

My mouth dry, I twisted on the flashlight, but couldn't see anything in either direction, just my fogging breath swirling through the beam of light.

The sound again, downstairs, then again a moment later only fainter, from behind me. I let out a breath; it was the original noise, reverberating and echoing around me.

It sounded like it was coming from *inside* the building. Someone walking, feeling their way around in the dark? More than one person?

I squeezed the pistol's grip, tiptoed cautiously down the stairs. I paused on the landing; crouching, looking. There was nothing for it. I descended.

My boots clamored, announcing my presence on the tiled floor of the lobby that linked the front and back doors of the building. There was a cold breeze, like a window somewhere down here had been left open. The narrow shaft of my flashlight beam pierced the shadows. I imagined that whatever was here was hiding in the shadows beyond its reach, retreating to another place, another world.

Times had changed and who knew what went bump in the night anymore? The attack on this city had brought out a kind of monster in all of us. I'd seen a smashed-in tunnel out of Manhattan, where thousands of people had been claimed by fire in a death worse than anything I could have imagined. There was still some heat coming off the smoldering plastic and rubber and fuel, and the smell sent me away faster than the sight. I'd run away fast, blindly south, the gun held high, wishing I could confront the people responsible for all this. In that moment, given the chance, I would have killed as many of those responsible as I could—and what did that make me?

Alone, standing here in a cold, dark, silent hallway.

The barricaded front doors held fast, but a chair I had stacked up had fallen over to the floor. The flashlight beam bounced off the glass and lit back at me, showing me nothing of outside. The wind tonight was strong and whistled through the broken window, rattling the mass of furniture. I pocketed the pistol and put the flashlight down on the ground to illuminate the scene before me. I walked forward to pick up the chair—

Stopped. Something, a noise or movement, a presence . . .

I waited for what was next, my hand searching in

the coat pocket for the grip of the pistol. My finger found its way into the trigger guard.

I pulled the pistol from my pocket.

Waited.

Nothing came. Not even a noise.

At least a couple of minutes passed while I didn't dare move, frozen in fear and expectation. I was prepared to scream and fight and shoot, but still nothing came. I could hear my heart slowing, my shoulders relaxing just a little—

There!

Something moved into the shaft of light; a rat, sniffing, bumping, making the flashlight spin again, giving me a quick 360 snapshot of the scene. Nothing else. Nothing but a rat. I almost laughed. I was alone down here.

I followed the animal out of the building and through the back door. As I inched it open, I was confronted by dark nothingness. The flashlight beam was lost out in the inky zoo grounds so I twisted it off, my eyes taking a moment to adjust to the night's gloom.

Clouds hung low, hiding the stars, but eerily backlit by the moon.

The animals. The cold wind. The unknown. The creak of a tree and the scurry of a critter. I remained in the impenetrable darkness, and walked a lap around the central pool, itself another level of black nothingness. There were perimeter fences here, made of stone and steel; I could just make out the ones that branched away from the arsenal building, but they were little more than a cursory deterrent. Still, I felt oddly safe out here, as if being surrounded by Rachel's flock of animals provided some kind of extra security; all those eyes and ears alert, ready to raise the alarm should someone enter their enclosure. But then what?

No Chasers had come in here yet, over the fences, so why would that change now?

Because they were getting smarter? Better at hunting? Better at getting at their prey?

I suddenly felt wide awake and full of purpose. I felt as though I could see better than any other night; farther, clearer, with more confidence.

I sat down with my back to the rear door of the arsenal building. It was my sentry and I was Rachel's. The animals too. We were a family, in this together. I pulled on my hood and felt warmth slowly spread around to my frozen face. I sat there for a long time, watching the scene before, waiting for dawn.

"Up early," Rachel said as she joined me on the steps, placing a hand on my shoulder.

"Couldn't sleep," I said; another lie. I could sleep, given the chance, forever. My legs and butt were numb from having sat out here for so long, but after all this time listening to the city's lonely beat, my mind was clear.

"Noises woke you?"

I looked up at her, suspicious. "Yeah," I replied.

"It's the building," she said, adjusting the brightness of her lantern. "It has a life of its own—tormented by branches against the windows, rats in the walls, possums in the ceiling, the heat and cold. And that's just the usual fare."

I nodded wearily.

"Come on in," Rachel said, wrapped tight in her blanket and her bed-hair tucked behind her ears. "You'll freeze to death. I've got some water on the boil."

I followed her inside. It was just before 7:30 A.M. Inside the bathroom I washed, using a bucket of warm water, savoring the heat and the steam. Through the bathroom window, I could see the bleak beginnings of dawn through the bare trees, whose branches shook in the breeze.

Rachel was stirring a pot of porridge on the fire.

"Thanks," I said, as she put a bowl of porridge with honey on the desk in front of me, juice and tea already laid out. I poured the pot of water into the teapot, jiggled the teabags.

We ate by the gray glow of the early morning light that spilled through the windows and Rachel sat quite straight while I tried not to slouch too much. The sounds of her sipping coffee, swallowing, her spoon against the bowl; all distractions from what I wanted to say.

All I wanted to ask right then was what it would take for Rach to leave. But I feared her answer. I'd either have to give her a good reason to leave, or this place would.

"Look, Rachel . . . let's leave soon, yeah?"

"We've got enough food for the week," she said, before reading my expression. "You mean leave New York."

I nodded.

"Jesse . . . you know I can't do that—I can't leave them here alone like that."

"But if I could find someone to take over?" Knowing that would be impossible.

She laughed. "Who? Who would you find?"

I drank my tea. "How about I bring Caleb here, to help out for a while—he's pretty handy, I think. Seems to know a lot about survival."

"He's just out of high school!"

"Well, I'm still in high school, and you're practically not far out of it."

"I mean, what, he's learned some stuff from computer games? From what you've told me he's a typical well-off New Yorker, probably never got his hands dirty in his life. You expect him to come here and shovel animal crap? Work all day in the freezing cold?"

"He'd help. I know it."

"We'll see," Rachel said, eating the remainder of her porridge in half-spoonfuls. "But . . . look, I know how you're feeling. I feel it too; overwhelmed, freaked, worried—about home, about family. But right now, my home's here. Maybe this is—you know . . ."

I stood.

"Jesse, I'm just being realistic. Have you thought that maybe this is all there is left?"

"I can't believe that, not after all that I've survived."

Her expression said that I should consider it.

"Somehow, Rach, no matter how I get there or what I find, I'm going to see home again."

21

It felt good to be up so early. I'd always felt so tired back at 30 Rock. Once or twice I'd tried sleeping more, getting up at the crack of noon instead of dawn, but it didn't help; I'd still felt weary. What helped was people—being around survivors like myself.

I packed my gear, dressed for outdoors, and took my backpack with me. I'd go to Rockefeller Plaza. I'd be on time, and I'd see if Felicity showed. Had she found my note? Maybe she was like Rachel, afraid now of leaving her home. The idea made heat rush up my neck. If she didn't show at the rink, I would swing past her apartment on the way back to the zoo. If I found her, maybe I'd ask her to go up into the tower at 30 Rock with me. We could scan the routes north and I'd get a chance to say a proper good-bye to the place, for good this time.

Caleb *would* help, I knew it. Maybe he wouldn't come here and shovel shit in the snow but I couldn't imagine him *not* wanting to help me persuade Rachel to leave. Maybe he'd resist the idea at first, for fear of the trek and the risk of venturing into unknown territory, but I had to persuade him so he could help me persuade Rach.

What else could we do? How long could they sit and wait for someone else to come help them?

My bag was empty against my back, reassuringly light on my shoulders. Everything about the day felt . . . *different*. It was the reassuring feeling that came with making choices and deciding my own fate.

I found Rachel in the Tropical Zone. So warm in here, a few degrees making such a difference. I passed her a walkie-talkie. She took it, looked at it strangely, flicked the switch and heard it crackle to life.

"I charged them at Caleb's," I said. "I'll take the other one."

"Take one?"

I nodded.

She knew then that I was leaving. She looked sick, sad, disappointed. She watched the river otters in their shelter. "Range isn't that far . . ." she said, distant.

"I know," I said, "but I'll take it, just in case. I'll turn it on each hour, say hi, just to see if you can hear me."

"Make it every two," she said, clipping it onto her belt, more sorrowful than angry, "on every even hour."

"I won't be too long, I just have to see if Felicity turns up."

"And if she doesn't?"

I followed her outside and looked at the sky, trying to get a read on the gray weather.

"Then I'll just collect some food and come back."

Rachel took off her coat, warmed by her work, perhaps signifying she was going to set herself into a higher gear now that it was about to be just her again.

"It's dangerous out there."

"I'll be okay," I said.

"Weather might get bad—you might get lost."

"I know my way around."

"You might not come back." She dumped some full buckets of water down hard and they splashed on the snow.

"Of course I'll come back."

But that hadn't been what she meant and we both knew it. She meant I might not *make* it back, that something might happen.

"You don't have to go," she said, looking down at the wet ground. "You can stay here, with me."

"Or . . . maybe you could come with me?" I countered, knowing she'd refuse but hoping otherwise. "Just a couple hours away from here?"

We stood there for a moment, the rhetorical question hanging.

"I've got work to do." She turned away and started preparing fruit and vegetables for the animals, her eyes wet.

At the synagogue on 62nd I turned off Fifth, walked east a couple of blocks and then south. It was nearing ten o'clock. I'd go to the ice rink then come back to the zoo. I'd bring more food; I'd cook for Rachel again—find a recipe and make her something good, work on convincing her to leave with us. She would love it.

I heard the distinctive flutter of birds in flight as I passed a smashed-in storefront. Pigeons, flapping out. The ceiling in the shop had collapsed, the hole going up through several stories. Remnants of what was.

A light dusting of snow covered Park Avenue. I walked faster, wide awake with hope and purpose, but knowing this feeling would fade. How it sapped you, this destruction, seeing death up close, always being on edge. Hope was a hard thing to maintain in the face of all that.

I stopped at East 59th to catch my breath and noticed footprints in the snow. I examined them closely. They were varying in size, and had obviously been left here earlier today. I counted them: at least a dozen people had traveled through here. They were divided into three distinct groups and seemed to be heading east. Maybe there was some kind of refuge, hundreds or thousands of people packed into the Bloomingdale's department store? I squinted against the sun, so bright against the snow, watching and waiting. I couldn't see anyone. I couldn't explore today; I had enough to do.

"... *stay here with me* ... *you might not come back* ..."

Rachel's words and their meaning rattled around in my head, with a kind of amplified guilt that came from thinking about her when not in proximity to her. It made me wonder if it were almost easier *not* knowing anyone. There was a burden in that kind of obligation. My mom had felt that, which was why she'd left Dad and me.

I pushed on, south, aware that if it really came to it, I may have to make a call on whether to try for the north on my own.

22

It was right on ten o'clock.

I rounded Fifth Avenue, past St. Patrick's Cathedral, between the buildings of Rockefeller Plaza, past the big statue of Atlas holding the world up on his shoulders.

I waited, catching my breath, at the eastern edge of the ice rink, or what was left of it. My hands firmly on my knees, my breath fogging, the sun bright behind me. I walked around, looked, watched, waited.

Is she here somewhere? Is she standing out in the open like me, or is she waiting, watching from afar, judging me before making contact?

I thought about calling out, but the sun went back behind dark clouds and it got colder, and then I remembered. I reached into my coat pocket for my gloves.

A figure approached from the shadows, becoming more distinct as it moved towards me, haltingly, and stopped.

Someone was standing there, a sole totem of another survivor here in Rockefeller Plaza. Alone. The person walked closer, and the sun peeked through the clouds for just a moment. I sucked in cold sharp air.

It was a girl, with the same blond hair and pretty face from the recording.

I'll be outside 30 Rock's entrance at the ice rink at ten o'clock every morning.

I paused, nervous. Was this is? Finally, we were both here. First Rachel, then Caleb, now Felicity. How many of us were left, here in Manhattan?

She walked closer. There was no doubt; this was the girl from the camcorder footage I'd found at 15 Central Park West—Felicity. She must have got my note and at last, I was here when I had said I'd be. She stood and looked at me, still uncertain. I waved and she smiled.

"Jesse?"

I loved her voice, the same voice from the recording. It was feminine and real and I wanted her to keep talking, to not stop. I hadn't felt that way about Rachel, which made me feel a little guilty.

I thought about the girls from the UN camp. Mini became my favorite of our group, and I knew that she liked me by the way she looked at me. But what I thought about most was what it had been like to be so close to Anna, the blink of her long, dark eyelashes, her bright red lips, the smell of strawberries. On our way back to the hotel at the start of our first week of camp we'd got caught in a storm. We'd huddled close under the awning of a deli and Anna kissed me and it'd been hot and fast. I'd wanted to be able to kiss her again but she seemed to forget all about the moment, and then it was too late.

"Yeah, it's me," I said to Felicity now, closing the distance fast. Fifty yards, thirty, ten.

I reached out with my hand, but instead she came in and hugged me. We stayed like that and laughed nervously at the simple joy of it all; a couple of survivors coming together. When she let go of me, she kept a hand on my arm as if I'd run away or disappear given the chance.

She was cold but her breath was warm against my neck. She stood back and I saw she had tears in her eyes. Her eyelashes held the wetness, her blond hair peeking out from under a knitted hat that held frost. Her smile was unbelievable. "And that's my dad's hat you're wearing."

"Sorry." I reached for the woolen hat I'd put over the Yankees cap.

"No, it's cool; it's yours now."

"Thanks."

She beamed.

"I'm sorry," I said. "I'm sorry I couldn't get here sooner."

"What do you mean?"

"I mean how I've not showed up here these past few—"

"Serious?"

"What?"

"Me neither!" she said, excited, her hands on mine. "This is my first! I went back home last night for the first time since I'd left—then I saw your note!"

"So you . . . you just got my message?" I was relieved; I hadn't let her down. The orange sunlight that bounced off the glass peaks of partly destroyed tower blocks was in stark contrast to a sky heavy with clouds. Powder snow began to fall and there was nothing but silence around us, two insignificant specks at the bottom of an abyss.

"When did you leave it?" Felicity asked.

I had to think about it. "Three days ago?"

"God, I was afraid of that!" she said. "I thought it might have been straight after I'd left!"

"I tried to find you in the park the day I found your video, but it was empty—that group were gone. And I felt sick coming here today, thinking *I'd* missed you."

"I must have just missed you at the park earlier that day," she said. "I saw that group of infected people standing around the fire and drinking from bottles—"

"Chasers, we call them."

She frowned and looked excited in the same moment. "Who's 'we'?"

It wasn't the time to talk about Anna, Mini, and Dave, so I told her about Rachel and Caleb.

"You're lucky," she said, "to have found people already. As for the Chasers, we must have seen that same group at different times."

"I know," I said. "So, I saw them right before you did, then you left that message and headed back out."

She nodded, still holding onto my hands. Hers were smaller, softer, warmer, even through gloves.

"Where have you been?"

"Trying to find other survivors," she said, "a way to escape this place."

"And?"

"I've been going out every day since, working my way from home to the Hudson, across through Midtown to the East River . . . I was trying to follow the water, to find a way out, but those people . . . were everywhere, sometimes chasing after me."

"You outran them?"

"I hid. I was so freaked out. Yesterday I stayed hidden from them in a café, one I used to go to all the time—they had the best doughnuts. I stayed there all night, in the basement. Before that I went to a couple of places I thought might be refuges . . . I was walking back to my apartment, I'd almost given up hope of finding someone, but then I came back and found your note."

I nodded. I could see how frightened she'd been all this time; just like me. Stronger than me, if I really thought about it. She looked at me and we seemed to share a moment: *Where do we begin?*

The snow picked up, a luminous dusting in the hidden sun's glow.

"Let's go inside someplace," I said. She nodded, smiled, and I knew then that I'd follow her anywhere. Question was, would she follow me?

23

I led us into the bakery I'd gone into the week before to escape from the Chasers. Inside, away from the breeze and the snow, it was warmer, and Felicity took off her scarf and sat at the counter. Everything looked as I'd seen it last, the counters and floor covered in ash and dust, the glass-fronted fridges filled with bottled drinks, the enclosed display cabinets full of moldy breads and cakes.

"Drink?" I asked.

"Water would be great."

"Water it is," I said and felt myself go a little red. *Why'd I say that?* It sounded so lame. Maybe I should have taken her to a cool bar, offered her a real drink. That's what Caleb would have done.

I handed over the bottled water, my cheeks flushing as she smiled and held up her bottle.

"Cheers."

"Cheers," I said. To be here, sitting next to her, her body heat close enough to be felt, looking out the window together . . .

"So," I said, "tell me about the Chasers—the ones that made you hide in the café?"

"There were lots of them, all running together. I didn't know what to do, so I just figured I should hide out until they'd gone. It was getting dark and I was scared; I didn't want to stay out there alone, but I knew I'd never make it home before they caught up with me, and I knew that bagel shop was nearby, so I ran down an alley, losing them."

She shuddered, and I could sense how frightened she'd been.

"They're not all predictable," I said. "The ones in the park are weaker."

"That group of them by the fire were leaving—I followed them down to a spot on the Hudson— they're in a building down there. I called out, but they just waved again, and I didn't want to risk getting too close. But it seemed, if they're like the others, that maybe they're getting better?"

"And who knows what's gonna happen after this, if it's the start of something new or the continuation of something old or the end or . . . whatever . . ."

"Jesse . . ."

"That's my name." *God, why did I say that? I should talk deeper, more—*

"It's a cool name. I like it," she said. "How old are you?"

"Sixteen," I said. *Should I have said eighteen? Nineteen, even?*

"I'm seventeen."

"Really?" *Damn. Maybe I should have gone with nineteen.*

"Yeah, really. What?"

"Nothin'."

"What is it?" she smiled, punching me lightly on the arm.

"Just . . ." I smiled back. She could punch me like that all she wanted, so long as she smiled. Man, that smile . . . "I thought maybe you'd be, like, early twenties."

Was that a bad thing to say, that a girl looked five or so years older than she actually was? Not for a seventeen-year-old, right? How the hell would I know? The only seventeen-year-old girls I'd ever spoken to were the older sisters of friends and they seemed to go out of their way to ignore me, all dating twenty-something-year-old idiots with tricked-out cars.

It was crappy being a teenager. Even though I had real company, I was still spending too much time living in my head and thinking too much. I wanted to be older and stronger and have more answers than anyone else. I wouldn't mind skipping a few years if it meant I could wake up tomorrow in my twenties and everything would be back to how things were. But I knew that was unlikely; everything had changed for keeps.

"It's cool, I get that a lot," she said, smiling more and looking into the middle distance out on the deserted white street. "Comes in handy when I go out with friends."

Like Caleb, she used the present tense. Maybe because this city was their home and it was too hard to put that kind of talk in the past, like it would never happen again. Whatever, I liked that she was closer to my age than I'd assumed.

"So," I started, desperately wanting to know everything. "What's your story? Where were you when—"

"The attack happened? I was home, doing some laundry in the basement." She paused, gathering her thoughts—or maybe pushing the still vivid memory a little farther away to make it bearable. "I thought it was an earthquake. I even braced myself in a doorway until the sounds died down.

"I stayed down there for ages, in that doorway, and when I finally went back upstairs and looked out the windows, well . . . that's when I saw people running. I don't know why I didn't rush outside—I just watched them. It took me nearly an hour to try to phone for help, but none of the phones, not even my cell, worked. TV, radio, all of it—gone. Then the power flickered off for good. All in the space of an hour, everything either destroyed or shut down, leaving me there, all alone. I sat at the window until it got dark, and then I sat on the couch and cried right through the night. I heard screams outside. I couldn't move . . ."

"Where were your parents?"

"They're away, thank God. We have a farm in Connecticut—they're there now, I hope." She paused, as though wondering about their possible fates, but snapped herself out of it. "My brother lives in Denver; he's in the Air Force, a medic. He's in Afghanistan right now, due back next month."

"What about your friends?"

"I've been trying to find them, any friends. Some of their buildings were destroyed, or their apartments were all locked up. Then I . . ." she slowed, "then I found one friend . . . her body, at least . . . and that made me stop wanting to look."

Her pretty face had turned pale and cold.

"Listen to me," she said, self-consciously, "talking about myself . . ."

"I like it; talk all day if you want." And it was true.

She blushed. "How about you? Where have you been these last two weeks?"

"The GE building at 30 Rock," I said. I told her everything that had happened over the past two weeks, the short version.

"These soldiers—what were they doing?" she asked when I'd finished.

"I'm not sure, they just had the two trucks, but said there'd be more. They said things would get worse, and that this virus is more serious where it's warmer."

"But, I mean, were they here to save people?"

"I don't think so. I don't know." She looked disappointed, just a little, but it was true: I didn't know and I didn't want to lie to her just to make her happy. "They drove on."

"And that's it?"

"That's it until this morning, when I headed out and—"

"And here you are."

"And here I am." *God, why do I keep repeating what*

she says? She's going to think I'm a class-A moron. I was eager to change the subject, to find out what she made of all this. "What do you think we should do? What do you want to do?"

"I'm not sure," she shrugged. "I didn't even know if anyone else had survived until I met you. I mean, survived and stayed normal."

I wanted to check something with her. "So do you think the virus was in the air? Do you think that's how the Chasers became infected? They happened to be outside when the virus was released on the city?"

"Must have been that," she said. "But the air's clear now, because of all that rain we had on day one, and all the snow since."

"So the only way it can be passed on now is . . ." I hesitated.

"By a Chaser physically infecting a survivor." She shuddered. "By . . . drinking from them."

"If that's possible, I haven't seen it—but who knows, right? We've got to be wary of that, of anything to do with them . . ."

"Well, I think heading north sounds like a good plan; maybe up to my parents' farm or something?"

I smiled. I imagined them, their farm, everything being how things were meant to be. How they might have news, real news, about all this. From there, maybe I could plan my way home. But I couldn't leave without Rachel or Caleb knowing. I knew then that whatever happened, I must not choose Felicity over my other friends.

"Is there anything holding you here in the city?" I asked.

She shook her head and sipped her water, but I could sense her despair at the thought of leaving. I could understand her need to be somewhere safe and familiar. I'd felt that way about 30 Rock. The call of home, the safety of the familiar, however misplaced that feeling of sanctuary might be.

"I just want to get to my parents."

"How about you come to the zoo with me?" I said. "See if we can get Rachel to come too."

"Sounds like she has her hands full there."

"But she can't stay forever," I said. "It's not safe, and it's too big a job. Maybe meeting you and Caleb will change her mind."

"But what if we can't get either of them to leave?"

"I think they will," I said. "It might take time, but they've both seen how dangerous these Chasers are."

"But don't you think Caleb's got so much here? It's his hometown."

She could have been talking about herself.

I thought about how Caleb spoke of his parents. Maybe he should go to their place to shock some reality into him—what was the likelihood that he'd find something as bad as, or worse, than he'd imagine?

"I think he's smart enough to know what's left, and to leave while he can," I said. "Rachel's hesitant about leaving the animals, sure. She wants to wait for help—she has to realize that it may never work out that way, and that things look like they're getting worse around here."

"Yeah." She knew what I was trying not to think: *Help may never come.*

"The hard part might be convincing her that things are getting worse," she said.

"We'll both need to explain it to her," I said.

"And if she won't leave?"

"I don't think I could leave her behind."

"Okay . . ."

"Okay?"

"I'll come and see her, try talking her around," she said, but the way she rubbed her arm I could tell something was up, something was making her uncomfortable.

"But . . ." I said.

"Huh?"

"What is it?"

She smiled. "I'm that easy to read?"

"You're like the third person I've spoken with in over two weeks," I said. "I notice everything. What is it?"

"Okay," she said, sitting forward. "This sounds stupid, I'm sure, but . . . I don't like zoos, never have. Prisons, really, don't you think?"

I was prevented from answering by a noise outside.

"What was that?" I asked, sitting up, alert, distracted from her confession.

"I was saying how I don't—"

"No, listen!" I said, and we sat there, still.

It was a familiar noise, but it took me a second to place it.

Felicity whispered: "What is it?"

"I think it's a truck," I said, and I was out of my chair, nose to the window, looking down the street. I could see movement and I felt the glass vibrate. "Those soldiers. They're back."

24

They passed our store, crossed West 49th, and went north. The big-wheeled truck rumbled over the debris of the collapsed building opposite us, its facade reduced to rubble that lay spewed across Sixth Avenue, the stenciled lettering on the cabin's door clear as it trundled by: USAMRIID.

"US Army!" Felicity said into my ear. "Medical Research Institute—they're like the military version of the CDC."

"They're the guys I saw the other day," I said, keeping low, peering out from the storefront as the truck climbed over the wreckage, two guys in the cabin and another couple sitting in the covered cargo area near the big container I'd noticed last time.

"Let's go and talk to them."

"No, wait!" I said, examining the soldiers more closely. My guy wasn't among them. "They weren't that friendly."

"But you spoke to them," she said. "Anyway, they're *US military*, Jesse. My brother has worked with them, they're good people: we've got nothing to worry about."

"Only one guy was all right, though. The other two wanted me gone."

"This is silly."

"Felicity, wait!" I said again, this time putting a hand on her arm to stop her leaving the store. "Please, let's follow them for a bit first, okay? If you're right, awesome. But let's just see to be sure."

She looked at me, then back out the windows to the truck as it wove its way through crashed vehicles, then back to me. "Okay."

Outside, I zipped up my coat as we ran to make up some distance. They were just over a block ahead, out in front of the Radio City Music Hall, when Felicity pulled me to a stop against an overturned bus.

"What?"

"Listen!" she said, a hand pointing up to the sky.

All I could hear was the sound of the diesel engine, reverberating off the buildings around us.

"Hear it?"

I was about to say "no," when I heard it too. A high-pitched sound, like a mosquito, and getting louder.

"What the hell is that?" I asked, scanning around, trying to work out what could be causing the noise.

"I saw one yesterday," she said, pointing up and to the south. There, flying at a height about forty stories above street level, was an aircraft. Long skinny wings and no canopy for a pilot. It was aimed straight for us. It looked like the glider that my dad had sent me up in for my sixteenth birthday, only this one was *sans* cockpit and had a motor of some sort, whirring away, growing in intensity, traveling fast, four blocks out, and then—

"Down!" I yelled, pulling Felicity to the ground.

An orange flash from under a wing pylon of the aircraft as a black cylinder broke free and streamed through the air, its heat palpable as it flashed over us and—

KLAPBOOM!

The shockwave shifted us on the ground, then the burning heat of a fireball and the concussive sound of windows blasting out and debris flying through the air hit us, in the same moment the aircraft buzzed loud overhead.

I looked up, coughing against the dust and rock fragments falling with the snow. What remained of the military truck was smoldering wreckage. The cargo area was gone and the cabin was a ripped-open shell burning bright with fire and making popping sounds. Black smoke plumed skyward. No one could be alive in that mess. The buzz of the attacking aircraft was fading, the smoke from the explosion now rising in two twisting vortices from where it had flown through the mushrooming plume—and then the noise changed as the aircraft ascended again, a fast buzzing gnat, soaring high over Sixth Avenue in what was apparently a huge loop.

"It's coming back!" Felicity yelled, her hand reaching out to mine. I was already on my feet.

"Come on!" I said, pulling her up and we ran east along 49th. The last thing I saw as we raced around the corner was a group of Chasers, the fronts of their jackets covered with blood spatters, in a crouched run: they were heading *towards* the wrecked truck.

We ran up Fifth towards the zoo. I constantly looked back over my shoulder, checking out Sixth Avenue, half-expecting to see that aircraft make a sweeping turn from a side street and zero in on us. I didn't see it, didn't hear it, and—perhaps more important—I could see no Chasers back there either.

We were silent, just the sounds of our shoes on the snow and our heavy breathing in sync and then a sound like a pop and everything went black.

Floating, the warm sun on my face, Dad cooking on the campfire, but now he's gone and I'm on the roof of 30 Rock. People running past me towards the edge of the building— it's the masses I saw in Felicity's video right after the attack; survivors like me. They're running away from me? No. I turn around and see, clearly, the threat: they're running from soldiers, men with the look and equipment and intent to do harm. I turn and go to call out, but too late, they've gone. What would I have said anyway? DON'T RUN? I run, fast as I can, to the edge and skid to a stop and look down— seventy-five stories and a blur of life below, hurtling to an end. Now they've disappeared, falling or fallen to the ground; they jumped to avoid being shot. I open up my fist to see a glass stone, small, dark and translucent; an irregular marble with swirls of gray, black, and brown, a childhood gift from an Apache American. "This stone holds the tears of my ancestors," he'd told me.

★   ★   ★

Then all I could see was gray. I blinked my eyes clear. The sky. Clouds low, clouds high—smoke. Smoke wisped and I felt heat and I turned my head to the side and a car next to me was on fire.

I turned my head, felt the cold snow on my cheek and the heat from the flames radiating to my face.

Felicity was there, between me and the burning car. Motionless. I scrambled over, pulled her towards me and her face moved a little, her eyes blinking.

"Felicity!" I said. She didn't change expression. I looked at her body, everything seemed fine but until she started moving, I couldn't be sure. I had an image of my friends in the wrecked subway carriage. I swallowed it down and looked around us.

Three other vehicles were on fire. Crackling and smoking, bright and dark. The street seemed deserted.

I looked down into Felicity's eyes, took her hands in mine. I touched her face, the back of my fingers down her soft cheek.

"Jesse?"

"Yes?" I said hopefully.

"I can't move."

I imagined her not moving at all, never again. I thought how I'd drag her to safety, to a building or the zoo if her legs didn't work, and then about whether I should even drag her if that were the case—I mean, if it was some kind of spinal injury . . .

"Wait," she said, her leg shaking. "See?"

"Are you doing that?" I asked, looking at her foot going side to side, then her knee bending.

"Not sure."

Her hands were heavy in mine, and I had them pressed against my chest as I knelt next to her.

"Try to—"

She squeezed my hands.

"That's it!"

I heard a noise—a whoosh of air—and a fireball erupted from a car nestled in among the wrecks. It lifted up from the rear as if the trunk had exploded and the sounds and percussion wave knocked me onto my back. I coughed and scrambled towards Felicity, who was rolling onto her side to face me.

"Can you move now?"

"I think so," she said, propping herself up on one elbow. I took her gloved hands in mine and she squeezed on tight, harder this time. I pulled her to her feet. She stood, unsteady, arms around me.

"I think I'm okay," she said. "Just a sec."

She leaned back and took a step down the road, unsure, a toddler taking baby steps. One foot in front of the other, a hand tight in mine, faster and surer as we inched away from the cars.

Another gas tank exploded, the sound of shattering glass from a building's facade as the fire belched and caught in the lobby, the force of the blast knocking us over. Plenty more to burn around here, and all this chaos sure to lure the Chasers. And just as I thought that, there they were.

Chasers. At least a dozen of them, headed straight for us, the burning mess between us and them, their forms shimmering in the heat haze.

★   ★   ★

"We have to hurry," I said. Even with her arm over my shoulders we were going too slowly.

"What is it?" Felicity asked, still looking dead ahead, stumbling, trying to figure out how to walk let alone run. She reminded me of seeing football players being knocked out and then trying to get up, all groggy on their feet at best—often they needed to be stretchered off. No time for that here. We had to *move*.

"The commotion's attracted the predators," I said, half-dragging her towards the next intersection. The smoke was carried with the breeze and followed us as we ran north.

She looked back.

"Just keep moving as fast as you can," I said, and we started what was a medium jog. She was making whimpering sounds.

"Come on, around this corner," I said, checking behind us as we turned again and rounded back onto Fifth Avenue.

"Where are they now?"

"They're at the burning cars." They'd just passed them. I could see glimpses of them through the smoke.

"In here," I said, dragging her into a clothes store. It was a big open space with a long curved ramp and white waist-high walls, twisting up a couple of levels. "Keep moving."

We made it up to the first level and I guided her down to the rear of the floor, navigating in the darkness. Through racks of clothes to a row of storerooms, change rooms, and a bathroom. I ushered her into the bathroom and locked the door behind us, which felt solid enough. It was pitch black in here and I could hear our breathing, so loud, and feel my heart racing. The dimmest glow of light under the door illuminated our feet and not much else.

"Do—"

"Shh!" I said. I helped her to sit on the tiled floor and lean against the wall. Another door in here led to a toilet. It was the same kind of door as the one I'd just locked, with the same kind of lock on it. If it came to it, if they found us and got through this first door, I'd put Felicity in there and make her lock the door and I'd fight it out.

Her hands found mine in the darkness and I sat next to her. Her hands shaking, mine sweating inside gloves. Bile rose in my throat, so bitter and sharp against my dry mouth. Her head rested on my shoulder and we sat in silence. If this is it, I thought, I hope it's quick.

At least two hours passed, seated on the floor of the dark bathroom, Felicity's warm body leaning against mine. I can pinpoint the moment that her heart rate calmed. Two hours in the dark, in silence, listening, before we ventured out.

25

As we rounded the arsenal building, I took the walkie-talkie from my backpack's side pocket, turning it on despite its being a half-hour before my scheduled check-in time with Rachel. Just as I flicked the switch and toggled the talk button, I saw her heading towards us from the equipment room, moving quickly as she always did, as if keeping busy would make time move faster.

"Rachel, this is—" I started to make the introductions, but then I noticed that something was wrong, something had happened. Rachel looked at me, worried, panicked; didn't even double-take at the sight of Felicity.

"Jesse," she said, jogging over and unlocking the gates. Close up I could make out there was blood down the front of her red polar-fleece jumper.

"The snow leopards," she said, tears in her eyes.

The snow leopards had been attacked some time overnight and Rachel had found them during her morning rounds, just after I had left. One was dead, the other was now sedated. Some heavy cut wounds down its side and back flank had been stitched up, the smell of antiseptic hanging in the air of the dimly lit veterinary room. Still, it was the most beautiful animal I'd ever seen.

Felicity stroked the cat's tail and turned to Rachel. "Who could do this?"

Rachel looked like she herself was feeling the pain of this leopard.

"Those *Chasers,* as Jesse calls them." She looked at me, hatred in her eyes.

"You're sure it was them?" I said, but I knew the answer.

"I found footprints in their enclosure. Man-sized footprints, four sets. They went into the pen last night or early this morning. I found some torn clothing and . . . this." Rachel held up a bloodied butcher's knife.

That was it, then. The zoo was no longer safe, no longer the fortress that Rachel needed it to be. She would *have* to leave now; if they had jumped the wall once, they could do it again. But I couldn't say that aloud, not yet. "I don't think Chasers use weapons," was all I said.

"But it had to be them—the Chasers—didn't it?" Felicity said. "Survivors like us wouldn't do this—I mean, what for? Food? There's food everywhere. Sport, for fun? No . . . Going up against these big cats with a *knife*? No way."

Rachel nodded. She'd already thought all that

through, but I still hoped the two girls would bond over Felicity's words.

"What can we do to help?" I asked.

Rachel stroked the animal's neck, its breathing shallow as it lay there on the cold table. She looked up at me.

"I'll need to care for her right through the night," she said. "Maybe do some X-rays to see what's broken, if I can."

"Anything you need, or I can do, I'll do it," I said. I wanted to tell her about the soldiers, about the attack, but this was her world and it was falling apart fast.

She looked at me as if she were trying not to cry. She seemed to hesitate, as if unsure of what she was about to ask. "What I really need," she said, "is a generator."

Suddenly, I saw the perfect way to bring Caleb here. I knew Caleb had a generator to spare. I also knew I'd need his help to heft it all the way up here. At last, the four of us would be together.

"That's easy," I said. "I can get one—I'll get it now."

Felicity said, "It's crazy out there, Jesse. Besides, we've only just got here." As if she was concerned about being left alone with Rachel.

"You've only just got back," said Rachel. As if Felicity wasn't even there. "You can't keep going, you've been up all night; you look exhausted."

I couldn't be annoyed with her. I didn't mean to exploit this situation, but perhaps the attack on her precious animals made Rachel realize that we were all in danger—that she couldn't go on for much longer without help. Her resolve was finally deserting her.

I shouldn't feel guilty, I tried to tell myself. I was doing the right thing. I could have stayed to help, to protect them, but then this was helping too. I hoped I was doing the right thing.

I said good-bye to Rachel, reassuring her that I would be back as soon as possible.

Felicity followed me out.

"Be careful," she said.

"I'll be fine. Just . . . just see where she's at."

"With what?"

"With leaving," I said, then felt guilty again. Was it cruel to make Felicity chip away at Rachel? But there was no judgment there in Felicity's eyes.

"I'll be back as soon as I can."

Felicity squeezed my hand through the bars of the tall gate. She'd watch over the wounded snow leopard while Rachel no doubt frantically fed and tended to the other animals. I made them load the zoo's rifle and have it ready, easily to hand. It was powerful enough to euthanize the polar bears if it came to it, so it would be more than capable of dropping a Chaser or two if they climbed the walls again.

What about four? What then? What if a whole pack of them attacked the zoo?

But it was Felicity who said, "Be careful," as she locked the gate behind me.

★   ★   ★

I went up the stairs to Fifth Avenue. No backpack, just me and my coat and the pistol in my pocket as I jogged south towards Caleb's.

My feet dragged in the snow. Were the Chasers as well organized as Caleb made out? Did they really hunt like that? Traveling in packs, with scouting parties out there? Could they communicate, call in their buddies when they found a decent feed? Maybe only at night, and that was why I hadn't seen that behavior myself. I'd seen them chase, but *hunting* people? *Planning?*

As I neared 57th and approached the bookstore, I saw more footprints, including some around Caleb's front door. I felt bile rise in my throat. Then I saw the blood.

26

In a panic, I banged on the glass door. The sun was really shining now, blinding, and squinting against the reflected white light sapped at the energy I thought I had. My head was spinning and I could feel droplets of sweat running down my temples. I heard a sound behind me and was relieved to see Caleb staring out at me through one of his black paper peepholes. He unlocked the door, all smiles, and gave me a big bear hug as I stood there.

"What happened?" I asked, pointing at the carnage, evidence of a fight out here at his doors. Was I leading Chasers and danger to my friends?

"They came last night," he said, looking at the fresh debris matter-of-factly.

"How many?" I asked, looking around me. No bodies, no sign of Chasers or anyone else—but no doubt, there were fresh footprints and marks out here, shattered bits of broken . . . something.

"Enough," he said. It was as if the matter was closed. "You all right, buddy? You don't look so great."

"I'm okay." I crouched down to examine the blood more closely. "So, how did they get in?"

He shrugged, scratched at the back of his head. He seemed so calm when I was so tense.

"Just after dark there was knocking at the door. I thought it was you."

"They knocked?"

"Yep," he said "Stupid . . . I opened the door without checking."

I swallowed hard, trying to catch my breath.

"Four of them, the kind with the dried blood welcome sign around their mouths," he continued, miming the ghoulish clown face with a finger motion around his lips. He stopped and followed my gaze; I was looking at his bandaged hand. "This? Oh, it's nothing. They rushed me, I managed to get the doors closed, and they would have bashed through if I hadn't run upstairs and pelted them with pots and pans and crockery. Then the riot gun when they moved out onto the street."

"Holy crap . . ."

"Yeah," he said. "Freaky thing is how they knew I was in here; I wasn't followed, I'm sure of it."

"So . . . what? They remembered you being here?"

"None have ever seen me come in here," he replied.

"Maybe they tracked your prints?"

"I'd been careful, and it'd snowed over. You know, I think it could have been those who followed us the other day."

"Serious?"

"Serious. I can't think of any others who have come here, seen me in here. Told you they're getting smarter." He was peeved. "So what are you doing here, Jesse, are you coming in or what?"

"Yeah, listen," I said. But I started to choke before I could continue. My throat was so dry and I felt hot all of a sudden. I moved away and leaned on a crashed car and coughed until I felt myself calming down, then looked through the windscreen and saw a frozen family of corpses staring back at me through long-dead eyes.

I run through the empty streets of Manhattan. The winter sun is out, warm on my back. I round the corner and the world is in shadows. I stop here, not wanting to enter into the impenetrable dangers before me. I could be in a tunnel, the light behind me calling. The snow here is up to my knees and I turn to head back—but they are still there. They are after me, nearing, getting closer with every stride. I am being chased and they will not stop. They're after me, or what's in me, and there is no time to waste, for to hesitate is to die. To die by their hand is a brutal way to check out of this world. Violent. Unspeakable. I have no choice. I speed into the darkness.

Black broken storefronts flash by me. I imagine I hear their footfalls but I believe it's my heart beating loud in my ears. This is a pace I cannot keep up for long.

Seconds later I am inside a building, the lobby of some formerly grand hotel, my shoes skidding on the ash-strewn marble floor and I catch myself against an overturned chair.

My breathing echoes, so loud. Like most other places in this city, this building has survived the attack but has been gutted by some kind of fire, the windows long blown out, debris everywhere.

I am out the back, on a silent street void of cars. The shadows here are long, stretching across and up the road, lonely flashes of sunlight between the teeth of buildings. I pause for the briefest moment and in that stillness I weigh up my options. I hear a scream of the chase and I resume running. I know my only option is to keep on running and hope that before I can run no more I find a place to hide.

Three blocks pass before I stop, hidden around a bleak corner, my hands on my knees as I catch my breath. My heartbeat drums in my ears, louder than I have ever heard it, as if it may be beating the last of what it can take or is spending all of its predetermined beats far too soon. My breath fogs as plumes of steam crashing through the still air in front of me, the frantic rhythm I've come to know well, always synched to the terminal sequence of heartbeats. I want to sink to the ground and rest, to catch my composure before they catch me. Just a matter of time, I know that. Something else I know: I know that when you run for your life, it is the fastest and farthest and fiercest you will ever move. It is, if you want to stay alive, the one time you have no choice. You have to run. Run!

When my eyes opened all I could see was a dim light.

I felt dizzy and my head throbbed.

"Jesse?"

I turned my head to the right. Caleb was on a seat

by the couch where I lay. He sat there, a bottle of water in one hand, his face concerned.

"Hey, Caleb . . ." I said, hoarse. I had something to say to him, something to ask, something urgent, but I couldn't place it. I tried to sit up, but it made me nauseous and my world went spinning.

"Here, buddy," Caleb said, holding the bottle to my mouth. I sipped slowly—two, three mouthfuls—then he took the water away. My breaths were deep and long, measures against the panic that was rising within me for no apparent reason.

What's bugging me? What's so urgent?

"How you feel?"

"Sick," I replied. I looked at him through half-closed eyes. "How did I— What happened?"

"You collapsed in the street out front," he said. "Knocked your head on a car on the way down to terra firma."

"Really?"

"Yeah. You've been out for a while. I was worried."

My head was heavy and I was so tired I couldn't even sit up straight.

"You look like crap," Caleb said.

I was glad Caleb was there to drag me in. *We're in this together, and we came together for a reason. We've found one another amidst all this.*

"Here," he said, rifling through some orange prescription bottles and presenting a couple of pills in his palm, "take these."

Taking those pills was the last thing I remember before falling asleep.

27

I turn and run. Upstairs.

The dark stairwell now lit by my flashlight, my feet finding their way and because the power has been out for over two weeks I am adept at moving like this, the sixteen-year-old me versus the eternal darkness. I trip and skin my knees. When your life depends on speed, accidents happen and you don't stop to sulk about it. The flashlight broke in the fall and I ditch it. I do not slow my ascent, feet a blur somewhere in the darkness until I get to the uppermost door. I am used to this now, this way of avoiding the chase. I'm a survivor, one of the few, uninfected, hunted. Preyed upon.

My hand finds the door handle. I open the door.

Daylight. This is the roof of the building. Several stories above the street, ankle deep snow. From the edge I cannot see them down there on the street or at the entrance and I know they must now be inside this building. Will they be smart enough to track me up here? Yes. When you are being chased, there are no doubts as to the ability of those who want to have you. They will get you, given the slightest chance. They don't use flashlights or even matches or a lighter—they will navigate those stairs in complete darkness *and they will do so better and faster than you or I, for their lives depend on this chase too. I reach around to the side pocket of my backpack and pull out the pistol. Heavy, loaded, ready to fire. How many bullets did it hold? Thirteen? Fifteen? I think thirteen. Dave's held fifteen.*

Dave. He was . . . I missed him. More than my school friends back home, maybe even more than my family. Dave, another guy my age, a friend I'd known for just a couple short weeks, a guy taken too soon by this place. I missed him, and I missed Mini, and I missed Anna—

Jesse! Someone called my name. Jesse!

Jesse, over here!

It's a girl's voice, so familiar, so sweet. As I hear it and it registers I know it should not be, but then nothing in this place is certain anymore. I turn—

Anna is there. Standing, by a handrail, waving at me. Beautiful Anna, my lost friend, here now . . .

She yells: Come on!

I run to her. At the edge of the building, where it backs onto another street, she's disappearing. The steel handrail of the fire escape snakes downward and I see that Anna is already a couple levels below, headed fast for the street.

I rush after her. I am halfway down the series of steel grate stairs when I hear noises from above and feel the vibrations of twelve pairs of feet thundering after us. I slip on the slick cold steel, tumble down to a landing, crushed of breath, but I get to my feet and push on, limping. Another flight, the sounds nearing behind me as I slide down what is a slim steel ladder to the street and turn to scan for Anna. I see her back as she rounds a corner up ahead—I chase after her.

I yell: Anna!

She's faster than I remember, faster than I'd ever given her credit for. When I get to the corner I see her across the street and she calls out to me before disappearing again and I chase after her, slipping on the icy road but somehow keeping my feet. In a few seconds I am running through the stacks of a library, headed for a light towards the back of the room and then I see them: my three friends. Anna is there, so is Dave, and Mini. I thought they'd left me days ago, I thought they were gone, that I'd never see them again. They smile. I have so much to say, so many questions and so much to share. Outside the window, the Chasers flash by, running fast down the wrong street. Then they're gone.

That was—

I stop speaking as I look across to my friends. I take a step back, taking it in—they've changed. Felicity, Rachel, and Caleb are now standing next to me, right where my departed friends had been. Had I imagined them just now, some kind of mind trick, some measure of madness? It's then I know that none of this adds up; the illusion is over, I know what this is.

I don't know what to say to them, the three people before me now. I am lost, more than just for words. My world seems to spin and I catch myself from falling by holding on to a bookshelf. My friends before me now, each of them a survivor like me, I'd met in the last couple of days. I'd met each of them in the days since I'd been alone, since the attack, since all this . . .

Am I dreaming?

None of them answer. The looks they give me—I could read anything into that. Pity. Fright. Ineptitude. Love. Anger. Anything and everything, to the point where I can-

not face them and I turn my back and look out the window to a day that is growing darker. I see Anna's reflection in the glass, her dark hair and pretty face and bright red mouth that tasted of strawberries. This may be the last time I see her like this, and I watch her, taking in this last moment in a string of final moments and we share a last look backward before going forward to the light: that pinprick of dawn, the horizon turning on itself, inverted, so that you are looking down at the earth and you're suspended up there, with the sun and the moon and all of us in the same big sky.

I know what this is. I know, and I'm sad about it. I know Dave couldn't be here, not like this, standing there behind me. Certainly not Anna. I know only one place where they could all appear like this, replace my other friends like that, so I know what this is. I've had enough and I have to leave, it'll drive me mad otherwise, it might even tempt me to stay with them. But something in me won't let me hang around and I think I'm grateful for that. This will all be over soon, and then I won't be alone anymore.

Anna asks: Jesse, what do you want?

I look at her reflection, and even though I'm asleep I cry in my dream and I can feel the tears in my eyes in my sleeping self.

I want what I've wanted every day since all this happened—I want to go home. But I know that's now not that easy, nor is that place so easily defined. I accept that home may now be wherever my friends are.

28

I opened my eyes and rolled to my side. I was hot, laid up on the couch, covered with a couple of heavy quilts, and weary, but there was something niggling away at the back of my mind. I stretched out to try to wake up, and kicked the covers off. Caleb sat next to me, writing in a book. I liked being here with him, but I could not shake the feeling that I had to be someplace else, that there was something urgent that had to be done . . . I just could not summon what it was.

"Hey, welcome back, buddy," Caleb said, looking at me.

I smiled sleepily.

"I've been talking to you all night while you slept," he said. "Hear any of it?"

I didn't answer, my world in a drowsy fog.

"Gotta say, you're a good listener; helped me figure some stuff out with my story."

"Story?" I asked, my voice raspy.

"Yeah, this is what I was talking about," Caleb said, showing me his notebook. It appeared to be some kind of graphic novel, evidently an epic judging by the size of the pad. "*Very* much a work in progress."

The cover seemed familiar: a cool but spooky emblem had been drawn in black ink on the gray-green card and it looked like a world that had burned, leaving a skeleton frame within, and there was a winged shield wrapped around the equator, all filled in solid with black. Was that winged shield protecting the world or attacking it?

"My villains are cannibals," Caleb explained, flicking though some pages. "That's just part of it, though. But they prey on people, hunt them, target them for all sorts of different reasons. Course, this is still concept artwork, but close to what I think it needs."

"Looks good." It really did. The illustrations were black and white but they were detailed, set out in a simple nine-grid layout against a backdrop that looked like near-future New York, emerging from the other side of all this mess. I thought about outside, about banging on Caleb's door and feeling sick, about fainting.

"These are inspiration," he said, showing me some open art books he had splayed before him on the floor. They featured vivid color pictures and they were spooky as hell, yet I couldn't help thinking perhaps my new friend was really more inspired by what had happened to this city in the last fortnight than the work of past masters.

"This one here is my favorite: *Raft of the Medusa* by Théodore Géricault."

The double-page color image depicted a handmade

life raft covered with the dead and dying, with some survivors sitting among and standing on top of them.

"It's . . . amazing," I said.

"Yeah," Caleb replied. "The picture, it was a French shipwreck in 1816, and the artist would visit the survivors in hospital to sketch and paint accurately—I mean, he even built a scale model of the raft. And he—and I'm serious—he kept a severed *head* on his studio's roof to sketch a corpse head! It's . . . sorry, I could talk about that painting for hours. I mean, even the way it's *composed* . . ."

I nodded, feeling a bit put off by his story and the scenes it conjured before me. They were creepily similar to what had been going on around us but in a sense there was something even more real about it than reality. Maybe it was the knock to the head. Maybe it was the pills Caleb had given me.

Maybe my lingering doubts about what was real and what was in my imagination hadn't gone away completely. Memories were all I had of some things— the memory of a happy family before mum left home was one I clung to. I wanted to get rid of some of them, of course—the bad memories—and I thought I could do that if I left 30 Rock. But that would mean surrendering all the good ones, too. Then again, I'd realized that even the most embarrassing ones or shameful ones—which I would have given anything to take back—were to be cherished. But perhaps the *lesson learned*—as if it were the title of one of Dave's books—was that none of them could be trusted. Or none of them was mine to control.

I stared at one of the other paintings, but found it hard to focus. There were some images from the Sistine Chapel that I'd seen with my grandmother when I was ten. They had been moving to me then, but they were haunting now; a reminder not only of perpetual gloom, but the reality of it.

"Why the hell cannibals?" I asked, feeling sick by the thought of it—too close to what was all around us now. "Couldn't you have some mutant space monster?"

"And what, copout with some giant squid coming in at the third act, destroying the city?"

"It'd do. It'd be better. It could still work as an allegory."

"Yeah, well I'm not running from this idea because of what's going down all around us," he said. "Since I was a kid, I've thought about this. And believe me, beyond all this Chaser crap, cannibalism has been around us—remember the news reports of that creep in Europe who advertised in a newspaper for someone to eat?"

I remembered that. It had really happened.

"Someone actually replied to the ad, right?" Caleb tapped the table. "There's good reason why they say that truth is stranger than fiction. My grandpa used to scare us with stories about a guy he worked with—another reporter at the *New York Times*—who had tried cannibalism out. I guess it stuck with me ever since, and when I started thinking about this book . . . it was something I wanted to write about, explore why it had stayed in my mind. Besides, what more evil a thing could I make up than something that was true?"

"People might not want to read this kind of thing anymore."

"I'm exploring this in my own way, looking for some answers, and to me that's art," he said. "Besides, my good guys will show you how the others can be beaten."

"And your heroes do what, exactly?" I asked, feeling slightly beaten myself. "Turn the bad guys into level five vegans?"

"Ha! No, but I might steal that line," he said. "They fight this underworld group—but it's hard, because these cannibals walk among us."

"Feeding on the weaker masses . . ."

"Yeah."

"And what, that's their secret? That they get power from whoever they eat?"

"There's more to it than that, but yeah. They have a litany of secrets that they live by, cannibalism being just one of them." He packed away his ink pens.

I looked up at the ceiling, my head floating on the pillow.

"But your good guys don't just go in and karate them about I hope?"

"Hell, no!" Caleb replied. "The better the evil, antagonistic force, the better the good guys—they've all in some way seen and felt the exhilaration of violence, and were distraught by the human consequences. That's why they were selected to defend humanity."

"Well . . . it sounds pretty cool, pretty solid," I said.

Cool and solid. Was it? What was I doing here, anyway? My memory came, short and sharp; a knife, in and out: *I had not slept last night,* but why? I looked at my watch: it was now the afternoon.

Was I just tired? There was more to this memory. Voices had woken me in the night—no, noises. I'd woken and gone out someplace cold, someplace old . . . the zoo! And slowly, my foggy mind began to clear, bit by bit. The girls were safe, they were together, but why had I left them?

29

I had a million questions but no time. Caleb was, as always, restless, ready to move on.

"Now you're awake," he said, "let's go outside for a while." He led the way up to the fourth-floor terrace, the roof of the store. I thought back to how those Chasers had come here and Caleb had pulled out his beanbag shotgun and gone: *blam blam blam*. That was cool. He was cool.

"Check this out." He passed me the binoculars. "That corner there, about five blocks down?"

I looked through the binoculars to where he pointed to the south. I was expecting another look-alike but there was not a soul to be seen. Everything looked pretty much the same: abandoned, crashed, smashed, lonely.

"After dropping you back at the zoo the other day, I was checking out a building on that corner," he said. "And do you know what? It had a *missile* in the front room."

"A missile?"

"Big one."

"Just laying there?"

"Like it had come in the window, smashed against the far wall, and didn't explode."

"Did it have any markings?"

"Like a 'Made in China' sticker or a DHARMA logo? No. Nothing at all."

We went back down the stairwell and onto the street, where I watched as he opened up the back of a van. He kicked out a ramp, rolled down on a motorbike, loud as hell. "How about it?" he said. "BMW 650 GS. Look at the tires. Chunky as hell, it'll get around these streets no problemo." He revved the engine. "Where's your spirit of adventure?"

"Skipped town," I replied. "Had to pack it away to make room for my spirit of survival."

"Just a quick ride?"

"They'll hear us."

"We can outrun them," he said. "Look, on my own, yeah, this is a bit dangerous, in case I have to stop, some Chaser creeps out of a nearby building from behind me . . ."

"See, my thoughts exactly."

"But you can keep an eye out."

"Or . . ." I steadied myself against the outside wall of the bookstore. My mind was still a mess, but I remembered Caleb and how he acted and how he was so full of denial. "How about you go check in on your old roommates?"

"Maybe," he said, then killed the engine. "Hey, where were you headed that day, on the subway?"

"The 9/11 Memorial," I said. "Have you been?"

"I didn't want to see it."

"You need to feel it," I told him. "Some things you need to feel." It seemed like the right time to say it.

"Why?"

"Because you've been marooned in that bookstore like I was up in 30 Rock."

He looked at me and even though I still felt spaced out, I could hold his gaze and I saw him soften. Finally, he said, "I can take you there."

"Can we go past your old place?"

"Okay . . . We can go via Little Italy. See if—if my friends are there."

I smiled at his change. I saw the truth, not a baby step but a leap. This wasn't about adventure, a reckless good time. He was starting to let the reality of this world in. He needed to see proof.

"How long will it take?" I asked, suddenly aware that time was important to me but I couldn't place why. I felt I had to see this moment through with Caleb, for his sake—maybe for both our sakes.

"Couple of hours," he replied, "tops."

I looked up the street towards the north. I still had a niggling thought that I couldn't place. He kicked out the bike's stand and got off. He saw my hesitation, and walked over to me.

"We can check it out another time," he said.

He put out a hand for me to shake and say goodbye. I looked at it, puzzled, wondering where else I'd go if not with him.

"Let's go," I said.

He broke into a huge grin.

★   ★   ★

The first few blocks were quiet. We took everything in, moving at a pace neither of us had experienced since the attack. The bike was sure-footed, the tires biting into the snow and ash, and we easily mounted curbs, rounded obstructions, zoomed down gaps between piled-up and abandoned cars. And we moved *fast*.

"I went for a ride just before, while you were still sleeping," he said over his shoulder. "Down along the Hudson. I met some other survivors. A group of them, down by Chelsea Piers . . ."

A pause, waiting for my reaction. I tried to focus, but it was as if there were a light hitting the inside of my skull and bouncing around. I knew the name of the place from the maps but I couldn't place it in my mind's eye.

"Survivors?"

"Yeah," he said. "But listen, this group—there are like forty of them there, in the big sports center. A few of them left when I got there, they were starting trouble, wanted a different existence to everyone else. They said it didn't matter what we did anymore."

I suddenly felt wide awake. "How so?" I asked.

"That— That choices aren't important because what's the point of life now? They were acting like this is now a world without morality, without consequences, so what's it matter what we do?" He glanced back at me quickly. "You know? Got me thinking: what if it matters even more now, what we do. More than we'll ever know."

"Yeah," I said. "I get that." But all I could think about was why he'd waited this long to tell me about these survivors. "Did any of this group know what's happened? Why the attack happened?"

"They all had an opinion," Caleb replied, "but apparently, on like the second day, a cop came."

"And he explained everything?" I asked.

"Well, he'd heard on his radio at the time of the attack that missiles were seen coming in, from the east."

"The east?"

"That's all this cop had told them, that there were sightings of missiles and it lasted a couple of minutes. Everyone had their own opinions on where they came from—Long Island, a boat, a submarine, Iraq, you name it."

"What about the cop?"

"He didn't say, apparently. He was there for a couple of hours and then left."

"Left?"

"They said he had family in the Bronx or something. Never saw or heard from him again."

"So what is this group of survivors going to do?" I asked.

"I heard a few talking about leaving, heading to someplace out of the city. But I guess most of them will stay. They say that more come every day, sometimes a few leave, but they're always getting bigger in number."

"Why didn't you stay with them?"

"I had to get back to you," he said. And then for no reason, he started laughing, kind of like my friend

Mini used to laugh. Her quiet, deep laugh always seemed odd coming from such a small person. But it was always contagious. Mini and Caleb were nothing alike and for a moment I was confused. I didn't know what to make of it, but started laughing too. Lately, I'd laughed mostly from relief that something worse hadn't happened. So it was nice to get caught up in the pleasure of it. We didn't stop until he started coughing.

"Besides," he continued once he'd recovered, "being around them reminded me how this is a weird city sometimes."

From Fifth Avenue onto West 14th and then down Bowery, which was clear, we moved like lightning. Caleb stopped the bike in the middle of the empty street and turned the engine off.

Up and down, the street looked virginal, hardly a vehicle to be seen, a blanket of white snow over most of everything. For a moment, I thought we could have been anywhere, anytime. Was I becoming used to life in New York after all? Would it eventually start to seem like home?

Caleb started the BMW up again and we rode south. At Hester Street he turned right and pulled up at the corner of Mulberry.

Fire had ripped through here, maybe on the first day. Charred buildings all around. We stood and I passed him the shotgun, which I'd had slung across my back during the ride.

"Wait here," he said, and before I could protest, he

headed down Mulberry on foot, disappearing into a building a few doors down on the left.

I walked away from the bike. Looked in some windows, most of which were broken. I saw rats, dogs, and not much else. In a parked car I found a briefcase that had a laptop, an iPad and a mobile phone, all with flat batteries.

This person had been to McDonald's—the massive drink container in the cup holder had slowly disintegrated out the bottom, leaving a sticky dark mess everywhere. A bag of food on the passenger seat stunk, but the burgers looked like they'd been made yesterday.

"Come on," Caleb called. He walked fast. From what I read on his face, I couldn't ask him what he'd found in his old apartment.

After a silent journey, we pulled up under the awning of a large brick building. Caleb kicked out the bike's stand and we got off.

"What are we doing?" I asked. We were still several blocks from the 9/11 site.

"I just want to see in here," he said. He entered the lobby of the Tribeca Grand Hotel.

Without stopping to see who might be watching I followed him through the doors. Inside the building was light, illuminated by a glass-roofed area.

Caleb walked behind the bar. Looked around. Then he rattled through some bottles and poured himself a drink. He sipped, drank, then poured another. He stared at it a while, I wasn't sure whether to look away or walk away, and then he looked straight at me. I walked over and took a seat on a stool, just the high bar separating us. Close up I could see that he'd been crying.

"I'll take a Coke," I said, giving him a chance to recover. "What are you drinking?"

"Nothing special. Not my favorite drink," he said. "That would be the Goombay Smash. Amber rum, coconut rum, apricot brandy, orange juice, and pineapple juice. And then the way they do it is with a little Meyer's floater on top."

"Why that drink?"

He smiled. "Memories."

My head did still hurt a bit, and I felt sweaty and my heart was racing, but that wasn't why I felt so weird. It was more that I didn't know how to feel about Caleb. I didn't entirely get him anymore. Was he always just messing around, or was it something else? Maybe there was more than the Peter Pan, fun and games side to him. Maybe I hadn't taken him seriously enough. I'd definitely seen a different side to Caleb today. Sure, he was still the carefree, good-time Charlie, but maybe all that was changing.

"Memories?"

"Yeah," he said, looking out at the big empty lounge over my shoulder. "Staying with friends on summer holiday of our final year of high school, up in Massachusetts. We went to this bar—The Beachcomber at Cape Cod. Everybody's happy there."

He smiled, lost for a while in thoughts that were so

happy it was contagious. I felt the summer warmth of that day.

"It's in a desolate place, at the end of a long road on these giant dunes, but once you get down there, it's buzzing. A live band. A sea breeze blowing through the screen doors to the terraced balcony on a swelter-ing day. An afternoon of laughing with friends. Mates, you'd call them, yeah?"

"Yeah." I thought again of my mates back home. "Your friend, back in Little Italy—he was there with you, at this bar, on that holiday?"

It was painful for him to remember, that much was clear. Maybe he couldn't muster the courage needed to venture into the apartment and see it—to *feel* it—to get answers. Was his friend in there, dead? Did Caleb assume his friend was now a Chaser, living the kind of life—if it could be called living—that he him-self said he could not bear?

Finally, he nodded.

"He loved it, he even worked there one summer. It's the kind of place where you're not going to run into door guys who are dicks. So much laughing, everybody's so laid-back. Didn't much care that we were underage. We'd watch the sunset. Bonfires on the beach every night. It was beautiful."

"There was a girl?" I asked.

"Yep. My first love, my first . . . you know. She was beautiful."

"What was her name?"

He shook his head. Something else lost or that he didn't want to share. I got that. I wasn't ready to tell him about Anna, maybe never would be: he wasn't that guy. I could be protective too.

"Caleb," I said, looking around the room. "Why are we here?" *Why was I here?*

"I miss all this. Look around. I used to come here. My friend's girlfriend worked at this bar, so it was easy, we'd kick things off here. The ambience, the life of the bar—that's the buzz. The chance that something unpredictable might happen, which wouldn't happen in your own home. That's why you go, right? Just because something may happen. The 'what-if.' Meeting someone. Being with someone. That's what I'll miss. No more names to learn, anymore, you know that? Do us no good to remember them much either."

30

Clean. Pristine. The 9/11 Memorial was like another world. We stood on an upper floor and looked out a window. The sun broke through a hole in the clouds—a gap of clear sky to the horizon that might make for a nice sunset, still a good couple of hours off. Caleb's eyes met mine: they were wet and searching.

"When 9/11 happened, I just sat there stunned," he said. "I think I was in shock those first couple of days, then bewildered . . ." He shone a flashlight on an image of the World Trade Center, just before the first tower fell. "It took a while for it to sink in that everything had changed."

All around us in here were the snapshots of the attack of 9/11, thousands of scenes of tenderness, images of loss and sacrifice, bookended by a wall-sized reproduction of a French newspaper's headline proclaiming: *We Are All Americans*. We all share in similar responses to this. Caleb was either angry or sad or probably both and then some.

"All the men on my dad's side of the family have

served in the Israeli army. All except me," Caleb said. I tilted my head, saw him sitting there. He looked like he was about to cry. "I never wanted to do that."

I simply nodded, as we looked at a picture of a fire crew.

"What have we done? What have I given? Nothing. Nothing but being one of the lucky ones to have survived."

"Are we even lucky?" I asked. I regretted my question for a moment, but Caleb looked at me as if he understood. "I think I know how you feel."

He looked out at the view, and said quietly, "What I feel is sick." His hands flexed into fists and out again, they were battered and beaten, kind of like how I imagined a boxer's to look after a big fight. "Or angry," he said. "That's a better word. I've been *angry.*"

I could understand that kind of sick, if it were a sickness. I felt it too, felt it run through my every fiber.

"When I met you, and up until now, you haven't seemed angry."

"Yeah, well, you don't know me otherwise, do you?" He looked at a picture of someone waving a bath towel from the top floor of the North Tower, illuminated now by our flashlights, there and gone again. He began to cry. I put a hand on his shoulder.

Caleb looked at me after a moment. "I am proud to be American, and I know . . . I know, I understand, that freedom is never free, yeah? It's earned. But I never thought it would be like this."

"I think everyone feels that way."

"It's different for me, though," he said. "After this 9/11 shit, when most Americans struggled to find something useful to do, some knew what was needed and they did it. Not me. I had nothing but fear, which got worse as we were plunged into war."

"And since then?"

"And since then our life has returned to normal—or, rather, some new version of normal. Gone are the days when aviation travel could be considered an adventure. There are long lines at ever more vigilant and intrusive security checkpoints and passengers looking at fellow travelers with distrust. Who's got a bomb in their shoe? Who's carrying a box-cutter? Who's what religion? I'd been afraid. I didn't want to go on to university or do work experience at a newspaper because I didn't want to know."

"Yeah, I think we're all like that to some extent," I said. "I think it's a self-defense thing."

"You agree with me?"

"Sure. Our generation has lost any real honest connection or commitment with our true feelings. We're rooting for ball teams, but we're not getting in there to play. Glued to the news, not caring. We're all so busy putting up walls around us—"

"*Were* so busy."

"Maybe."

"No maybes," he said, walking, not mad at me but frustrated by it all. "Look around us, Jesse. This place in here, this memorial—what it symbolizes—and look at it! It's *pristine*! Not even a scratch. How's that happen? Irony?"

"Maybe this place was designed that way, to withstand—"

"It's more than that, and you know it." He stood by a window and looked out at the two big square pools that marked the footprints of the Twin Towers. "We're a generation of spectators, no doubt about that."

We watched Chasers, the docile, weak kind, down by the water. Thirty, maybe forty, of them. I had been wary yet respectful of them before, but now Caleb had me scared, as if I were Scout and maybe he was Jem and the Chasers were a bunch of Boo Radleys. I smiled at that. Would they all prove friendly, in the end? Would I realize that I just feared what I didn't know, and feared what fear itself conjured up in my mind—always the worst? It drove me crazy to think about it.

"Were," I said. "Were a generation of spectators."

Caleb grinned.

"When we met," I said, suddenly remembering the moment with clarity, "you made that point about not killing them, the Chasers."

"They're people."

"Yeah, I know," I said, my mind flooding with jumbled images. "But . . . what if you had to? Could you kill one?"

"I don't know." He rested his forehead against the window. "Can I ask you something, then, as my last friend around here?"

"Of course."

He looked out at the Chasers. Some were on the ground, dead or dying, but then they were all dying pretty fast, with little hope but the immediate, of keeping at sipping away their thirst.

"If I turn out like one of them," Caleb said, "I'd rather be dead. I'd rather be dead than a Chaser, or anything like them. Understand?"

I couldn't answer, so I didn't say anything. I watched the reflection of his face in that gray light of the gloomy day.

"You gotta. It's all I ask," he said.

"I don't. I can't."

"You do," he looked at me. "It's the contract you signed when you became a survivor on this new earth. The stakes are raised now, buddy. The time comes, you gotta step up to the plate, no matter what. No more spectating."

31

Back at the bookstore, I stood in front of the bathroom mirror, leaning on the basin. There was a dim shaft of light filtering in through the window. It reminded me of the light in the subway tunnel, when I'd come to after the crash and emerged into that Manhattan street; the scene that proved my life had changed forever. I looked at my reflection, my face cast in shadows that highlighted my sunken cheeks. My breath steamed in the cold. I used some wet paper towel to clean my face, washed the dried blood on my forehead from when I'd collapsed earlier.

Seeing a bottle of pills on the shelf, I remembered the medicine I'd taken. It must have been strong to have such long-lasting effects. I called out to Caleb, "What were those pills you gave me?"

"Pain and sleeping pills—you were delirious," he called back. "You okay now?"

"Yeah. I guess so. Did I say anything, before I hit my head?"

"You'd just run here, you were out of breath."

"Yeah, I remember that . . ."

My ears were ringing, but a new sound cut through—I could hear Caleb starting up the generator.

Generator!

"Caleb!" I yelled, bashing through the door into the storeroom where he'd set up the generators. He wasn't there, but the engine was running and the exhaust jerry-rigged up through a makeshift pipe into the ceiling cavity. I raced out to the café and slipped over in my socked feet on the tiles.

"You really gotta start slowing down before you get yourself—"

"Caleb," I said, getting up, "we gotta go!"

"Where's the fire?"

"The zoo! We have to get there!" I told him about the wounded snow leopard, how Rachel needed a generator, how *that* was the reason I'd raced to the store.

"That was yesterday!" I said. "They needed it yesterday!"

Caleb looked at me, weighing up the pros and cons of my proposition. Things seemed to bother him less; he was able to deal with all that had happened to his city. He'd been as alone as me since the moment of the attack, yet looking at him now he seemed the stronger, the more capable of the two of us. Whatever Caleb's decision, I suddenly knew with certainty that my idea of him had changed forever—he saw this city for what it was.

"Come on, then," he said, and I could have cried with relief as he stood. "Let's go."

*   *   *

I looked down the slippery stairs. My legs were shaking from the strain of having pulled the generator along the road from Caleb's. We'd used ropes tied through the tubular steel frame, and some laminated book posters as a makeshift sled. Every few paces it would catch on debris; it was heavy work.

We turned the generator around, pushing it to the top of the stairs so that it balanced at the edge. For it to slide down out of control, for it to tumble down and smash just didn't bear thinking about. I made sure it was in no danger of slipping away of its own accord while Caleb went back to the street, cleared out the gutter with the heel of his shoes and hands, the snow and dust and debris in mounds at the side.

"I'll anchor it and play out the ropes, you guide from there," he said.

I stood by the generator, looked across the sidewalk to the cleared groove several paces away.

"Yeah, that should work," I said out loud.

The generator teetered at the edge on its makeshift slider. The ropes tightened as Caleb backed across the sidewalk and sat down on Fifth, my own legs straight out towards the gutter in a brace. Slowly, he let out the tension and so did I, and the generator started to move. Caleb gave the ropes a flick as if they were the reins of a horse—and the generator was off, fast, the friction burning my gloved hands until we took control again to slow its descent and finally the rope was slack.

At the top of the stairs I stood and shone the flashlight beam down; the generator had arrived safe and sound. Caleb bumped in close next to me. We had made it, hopefully in time. Slowly, we, too, made our way down; my legs wobbly, my head throbbing, my hands aching, my heart fluttering with a whole bunch of *"What ifs?"*

32

As soon as the generator was connected up, the three of us helped Rachel move the sedated snow leopard onto the X-ray bed. It took about an hour and by the end of it Rachel had splinted and bandaged the animal's hind leg, and we put it into the recovery room before making our way back inside the arsenal building.

After that, it was time to talk. As with any group, we sized each other up, formed and withdrew prejudices. Of course, I didn't know exactly what everyone thought of each other. Maybe that wasn't necessary; everyone was being forced to act differently from their normal selves, anyway. What would they have made of me if we'd met at the UN camp before all this happened? I'd even thought Anna, Dave, Mini and I would get cabin fever and tire of each other—would that have happened? Would my new friends and I still be on good terms throughout the days, maybe weeks, it would take to reach safety? If I made it back to Australia, how would my old friends treat me? Would we get along like we had before, when everything had changed?

These were big questions—too big. For the moment, I was happy to feel a sense of pride that I had managed to bring everyone together. But what if it didn't last? If I doubted Caleb, how much could I expect the others to trust me? Would a natural leader emerge once we got going? Did my friends feel as responsible for me as I did for them? I remembered feeling the strain of that before—how it eats into you and makes you doubt yourself. But more than ever, uncertainty was the last thing we needed.

I listened carefully to the conversation, not just for the soothing spirit of togetherness, but listening out for where we agreed and where we didn't.

"Remember what happened in New Orleans after Katrina hit?" Rachel was saying. "How long it took for help to properly arrive there? For law and order to be restored? This is bigger than that, maybe this will take even longer . . ."

"That could be what that soldier meant, Jesse," Felicity said, "when he said it was worse elsewhere, that things here weren't that bad, not yet."

I watched her face as she spoke.

"But we all agree that things are worse since then," I said. "The Chasers are—"

"Getting a hell of a lot smarter and better at what they do," Caleb finished.

"Might be worse everywhere," Rachel said. "If a neighbor-against-neighbor kind of thing is going on in the warmer areas, I don't want to see it firsthand."

Felicity and I shared a look and she gave me that smile of hers; it would still take some persuading to get Rachel to leave. Rachel hadn't thanked us, hadn't made a big deal about us bringing the generator or even about our late arrival, yet there was a shared, un-spoken feeling of having achieved something good, a sense of better late than never.

Caleb got the fire roaring and Felicity and I organ-ized some food: a big batch of pasta with tomato and olive sauce. Rachel cleaned herself up, returning as Caleb pulled out a couple of bottles of wine, juice, and one of vodka, and a selection of cheeses and boxed chocolates from his backpack.

"My contribution to tonight's meal," he said. "Oh, and this."

He set up a little battery-powered Bose speaker sys-tem and docked an iPod.

"Sorry, it's on random," he said, hitting skip. "Rocket Man" by My Morning Jacket came on.

"Nice track," Felicity said. "Feel free to come over for dinner again." Her eyes sparkled and I had to stop myself from staring at her for too long.

Rachel sat by the fire, towel drying her short hair. I contemplated apologizing for my lateness but she seemed over it, or maybe it was a bigger deal to me: we'd got here, with the generator, and that's what mattered most.

I set four places at the desk and brought in another couple of chairs. Caleb poured drinks and Felicity set down the pot of pasta. The warmth of the fire and the sound of the music, it was as normal a scene of life as I could have imagined, and it brought memories from a better time flooding back.

Four places. We were all here. My wildest dreams of achieving a community had come true in a few short days. I started to doubt why I'd want to leave this city and risk breaking us up, but I knew it was what I had to do. It was what I had been working towards—home.

Caleb told the girls about the group of people he'd met at Chelsea Piers. I felt pleased to have known about it before them, it meant I could follow the girls' interest.

"So there *are* other survivors out there!" Felicity said.

"Must be a lot more, I reckon, people hiding out in buildings and stuff," Caleb said.

"And, these ones at the Piers, they're all friendly?" she asked.

"Friendly enough," he replied. "Though they'd seen plenty of looting, especially in the first few days, before the true reality of the events settled in."

"Are they going to stay?" Felicity asked Caleb.

"Not sure," he said through a mouthful, then swallowed and drank some more wine. "Some want to leave, see what's out there, but most I talked to seemed to want to stay. They've got a few sick, a few kids, so it's tough to just pack up and go, yeah?"

Rachel nodded, Felicity topped up their glasses. I popped a bottle of mineral water instead, the comforting food and warmth of the room making me sleepy enough.

"They didn't know what happened?" Rachel asked, plating up some more food for us all.

"They've all got their opinions," he said, "but I didn't hang around that long to talk to everyone at any length. The general consensus was that it's some kind of eschatology."

"Some kind of what?" I asked.

"The final events in history, or the ultimate destiny of humanity."

"Commonly referred to as the end of the world, or the end of days," Rachel said, seeing my and Felicity's blank faces. She was holding her glass of wine in both hands, her elbows propped on the table, the warm glow of the fire on her face. "I took a theology class in college. I think it's defined as the four last things: death, judgment, heaven, and hell."

"So, what, they're a religious group?" I asked.

"Some of them, yeah," Caleb said, wiping pasta sauce from his chin. "It's getting them through, whatever they believe."

"This is an apocalyptic time," Felicity said. "The end of . . ."

"An age," Caleb finished for her.

"But some want to leave New York, right?" I asked.

Caleb looked to me. "Yeah, but they're gonna try and head south," he said, turning to the others, "which Jesse, here, thinks is a mistake."

"That's what that soldier, Starkey, told me," I said. "But who knows?"

Caleb said, "I said to Jesse that I thought those soldiers, or whatever they are, may have been there to loot."

"I don't think so," Felicity said. "We saw one of their trucks this morning. USAMRIID—they're a scientist outfit, specialists in virology and combating biological warfare."

"You seem to know a lot about them," Caleb said.

"Only who they are. My brother's a medic in the Air Force, he's worked with them," she said. "They're here to investigate this biological agent, I'm sure of it."

"But why would their truck be attacked like that?" I asked. "I mean, who would attack it?"

No one had an answer for that.

"Look, I think we should make a decision, though; one way or the other. There's four of us now. We can't just stay here, especially now those Chasers are getting so . . ." I trailed off, seeing panic cross Rachel's face. I looked to Caleb for support. "Maybe we should at least head to the piers? See this bigger group?"

He shrugged and nodded like it was a possible scenario. He turned to Felicity: "Tell me more about this aircraft that attacked the truck."

Felicity described to him what we'd seen in the street, how the aircraft had come in fast and fired a missile. The two of them talked while Rachel left the room to go check on her patient and I cleaned the dishes.

"Do you think this will get worse?" Caleb asked Felicity.

"Outside of us, of this little group that Jesse has brought together," she said, "it's getting worse every moment. Jesse's right; our best chance of survival is to get out of this city."

33

I woke up in a cold sweat and with shocking, aching clarity. I sat up on the rug and my head spun so much I had to sit still, not move, wait for my world to stop revolving and the stars to clear from my vision. The room was dark but for the glow of the fire. Total silence. I was at the zoo—I'd made it back, and I remembered having dinner with my friends and talking in front of the fire.

How long had I been asleep? I looked at my watch—five minutes to midnight. Where were the others?

I put my feet to the floor. My T-shirt was soaked through with sweat, my jeans too. I was hot and cold at the same time. I stood, leaning on the chair in front of me for support, and pulled on my jumper.

"Caleb!" I called. "Rachel?"

I walked over to the door, opened it and listened. Nothing. I checked out the window and saw Rachel and Felicity talking in the moonlight as they crossed the grounds to the vet room. Caleb was nowhere to be seen.

I went to the bathroom and splashed cold water on my face.

"Caleb?" I called into the hallway. Downstairs: "Caleb?"

Nothing. He'd gone. I should have known he wouldn't stick around, that he didn't want to be part of our group. Or of any group, maybe.

But I needed his help—we all did if we wanted to escape and find the other survivors, those down at the piers. I noticed his shotgun was gone, his heavy coat too. He was out there, somewhere. I went out to the vet room where Rachel and Felicity were tending to the snow leopard.

"He left about half an hour ago," Felicity said in answer to my question.

"Where'd he go?"

"I don't know."

"His parents," Rachel said, adjusting the IV drip in her sedated patient. "That's my guess."

"I have to find him."

"It's too dangerous," Rachel said.

"It's dangerous for him—"

Rachel looked up from her patient, concerned. "Jesse, don't be stupid, it's pitch dark."

"I'm not being stupid," I snapped back, and then more gently: "I'll be careful."

"You won't find him like this," Felicity reasoned. "Why don't you wait for morning? It's not too far off."

I turned to face her. She really was pretty, even with those dark shadows under her eyes. "I think he needs me to do this," I said quietly.

"He was drunk," Rachel said.

"Then all the more reason for me to go and make sure he's okay."

"Do you trust him?" she asked, in a tone that made it clear that she didn't.

"Of course." I tried to sound more confident than I actually felt.

"Do you believe what he told us?" Felicity said. "About that group of survivors?"

I could see that the girls had talked about this and had their suspicions.

"I do. We all need to," I said. "That group of people might be our best chance of survival."

After a moment, Felicity backed me up. "He's right," she said. "We need Caleb if we want to find them, you know that, Rach."

I couldn't stay a moment longer, there was possibility in the air: if we could meet up with this group, I might just be able to convince the girls to leave.

I went back to the room we'd sat talking in last night and found Caleb's big map of Manhattan, another half-empty bottle on top of it.

He's out there, toasted, armed . . . but doing what? And why? He knew we were going to leave together tomorrow, what couldn't wait?

I took one final look at the map. It was covered in his scrawled notes. There was a big black cross drawn alongside Fifth, down south, past his bookstore, with the annotation "missile seen here." I remembered him explaining it, how it was unexploded. Then, next to the cross in a different-colored pen, there was another note, written small. I adjusted the flashlight beam to read it: "Maybe this is what those army guys are after?"

Is that where he's gone? At midnight and by himself? It made no sense.

Had he *really* met a group of survivors at the Chelsea Piers or had he just craved their existence, willed them into being in his imagination? I recognized some of myself in him, how I'd been those first twelve days. I'd filled the time, I'd made do, done my best to keep sane. Caleb's denial was palpable. There may have been no sinister undertones, no "black dog" in the distance, but I knew something was amiss. Maybe he let it all out in that notebook, that graphic novel. Maybe that was his secret.

I couldn't understand him, but I had to trust him.

He was my friend, and friendship now meant more than anything. Still, I banged my fist against the wall in frustration, then again and again until I could really feel it. Another day consumed by this place.

I sighed and started to fold the map, but just as I did I noticed something new, something that stood out for its black circle of permanent marker in the Upper East Side. There was a word, a single word written in clumsy, drunk handwriting: "Mom." His parents' house.

I headed north, alert, wary, towards Caleb's parents' place. There was almost no breeze, and the streets were full of noises I hadn't noticed before—a shift of rubble or debris, the creak of a piece of broken roofing. Little, tiny noises that cut into the silence.

The UN building was close to here—it might be gone, it might be burned out. All those people I'd met and spent time with on this camp, gone. Or worse: still there, dead, frozen, broken. I avoided going there with my thoughts. I wanted to go on remembering that place and the people the way I did now. Like Caleb did with his parents. Had I pressured him into thinking about them, into seeing them? What would he be like once he saw what had happened to them? Surely this reality around us was worse than anything we could imagine.

I realized with relief that the UN building was to the south of here anyway, and that I wouldn't have to pass it. Thinking about it made me curious, but I had enough on my mind as it was; I could wait to hear about the fate of it and its occupants.

At the block between 59th and 60th it looked like a big airliner had tried to land—there was a jet engine in the middle of the road, as tall as me. The buildings either side of the avenue were shattered for two whole blocks, north to south. They were blackened shells. I couldn't tell if the aircraft was commercial or military—it was wrecked, smashed to shreds, the paint burned off down to bare metal fuselage and the skeletons of the wings. I trudged through the wreckage, trying to find a clear path across, but the snow was thick; it gave way to reveal hollows where debris had created cavities. Too dangerous.

I turned to find a way around.

Chasers.

Four—no, six of them. A pack: six men, not much older than me, but gaunt, malnourished-looking in the dull moonlight, with dark rings around their eyes. Had they seen me? Had they been following me just now? Tracking me? Hunting me? Our positions on the food chain were clear and I had no choice but to act like the prey that I was: I ducked down low and ran.

34

Terrified. Petrified. Stupefied. I hid among the wreckage, not far from where I'd seen them, and was still, as still as I could be. I dared not breathe. I could see a frozen arm before me, sticking out from the snow. It was the color of the night sky. I started to retch, something I'd recently discovered I did when faced with utter fear. I did everything I could not to vomit, to remain silent. The back of my throat itched. My eyes ran with tears.

I felt them nearby, felt their movements around me, heard their shuffling, their murmurs. A piece of aircraft, wing or fuselage less than a hand's span thick, was all that separated me from them.

I closed my eyes and listened, tried to place every one of them with my ears. One, two, three, four . . . Were there four or six? They could step around and I'd be trapped, my back against this cold metal sheeting, with no way out.

I remembered a movie about a plane that crashed on a remote snowy mountain in South America somewhere, the Andes maybe. It was based on a true story, and the survivors of the crash had to eat the bloated, frozen corpses of the other passengers to stay alive. I wondered if Caleb knew about that? Many of those who survived the crash succumbed to cold and injuries. Those who lived through the ordeal had only done so by eating human flesh. For more than two months they were up there in the freezing mountains, alone.

Behind me, the noises of the Chasers were becoming slightly clearer; muffled shuffling, heavy breathing. I was gripping this piece of fuselage—part of a wing, I think—that was balanced on a steep incline, and I had to be careful not to slip, the ground below had been gouged out and a deep puddle of filth had filled it. I was shielded here from view, the wing hiding me in the shadows of the carnage.

The longer I stayed, frozen to the spot, the more details emerged about the scene that spread along the street. This was like some kind of mass extermination rather than a plane crash; nothing was an accident on this new earth. Aircraft didn't drop from the sky into a dead city like this—did they? Had they been in transit and not known what had happened here, did they eventually run out of fuel and try to land? No. I bet they'd been shot down.

I'd seen and heard fighter aircraft in the opening days, even on day twelve.

It would be so easy to direct my violence at the Chasers, to go back to 30 Rock or Caleb's and tool up with some serious weapons, then cruise the streets, shooting them one by one, for keeps; to lessen the danger with violent acts of my own. I could kill with the best of them. I could feel entitled to do so because I knew who I was: a survivor. A goddamn survivor. Who the hell were they?

I had dreamed about one Chaser I'd seen from 30 Rock. I saw his face in so many of those bloodthirsty, opportunistic others. He was a symbol for what I feared. For all I knew, that Chaser was already dead, but his face was burned into my memory. *The enemy is this germ,* I had heard Caleb say. Maybe, if it came to it, I could beat that Chaser. But a germ?

I zoned out, meditated myself away from the noises, from what I imagined were mouths closing over flesh. I pictured Caleb here with his huge shotgun, blasting away at these monsters one after another, but then my thoughts spun out of control and I realized the Chasers were coming thick and fast—out of nearby buildings, up from the subways—an endless supply, until there would be so many of them we'd be overrun.

Damn this place. Damn it and all it contained.

And, most of all, damn whoever did this, whoever carried out the act leading up to this, all those responsible. Billions of cells of human beings, reduced to just another form of carbon. Why would anyone have done this? What a waste.

I wanted to be anywhere but here.

I stayed there, still, for fifteen minutes or more, moving myself around so that I had my back to the fuselage, the cold aluminum no longer burning my bare face.

I scanned around, searching the shadows for movement. I heard nothing around me; there was nothing but empty space. I was alone. I let myself slide down to the ground, where I fell in a heap. I sat there on the ledge, my legs hanging down, my toes near the filthy bog below. My arms felt like dead weights, hanging useless by my sides. My legs were asleep from being wedged at such an angle, the fingers on my left hand were red and swollen and my palms ached with cold. My hands shook as I looked at them, bare, and I put my gloves back on. I stared at the emptiness surrounding me, listening. The rustling of animals nearby—I saw a dog shoot across the street, followed by another. The *crack-crack* of a couple of distant rifle shots to the south.

I headed east, to distance myself. The night was clear and the moon was out. I passed a burning apartment block on Lexington and 71st: a five-story signal fire. Flames licked from the windows, belched out the front door in rolling splendor. It soon spread to its neighbor, a cancerous cell. I used the light to check the map: Caleb's parents' house was on the next block east.

There were two people about fifty yards away. I couldn't be certain whether they were survivors or Chasers, but I saw them watch the fire, take turns to drink from the gutter like animals and my suspicions were confirmed. I had the Glock in my right hand. I could not feel my left hand. I could not feel anything.

Turning to look back down the street, in the warm glow of that fire, I could see those two desperate Chasers. They were standing where I had been, watching the flames, feeling their heat. Little separated us. My heart sank and I knew then, as I had known before, that I would never preempt violence.

I kept moving, flicking on my flashlight to check the numbers on the green canvas awnings over building entries. Looking for a sign of my friend, in one of these buildings, somewhere here.

Building after building, lobby after lobby, was empty, the street barren save iced-over wrecks and lumps of snow covering the dead.

Is this where the world ends? Is this how? Does it just snuff us out, one by one, until there's just no one left?

I tried to snap myself out of thinking this way. The cold was getting to me.

I walked on south, trying to stay alert, remembering that we would all leave this place, head north, away from all this.

A noise. Something breaking, glass maybe, in a building across the street. I ran over, my flashlight off, my back against the wall as I closed my eyes and listened to the sounds in the lobby.

That face from two weeks ago, looking up at me after he'd drunk from a warm body, flashed through my consciousness. That face I could never forget. Perpetual evil, death at my door.

The chill of the brick wall crept into my bones. Everything became silent and I looked back up the street at that glow of the building fire. I took a deep breath, and armed with my flashlight and pistol, I moved away from the wall and looked around the doorway into the lobby—to come nose to barrel with a gun.

"Please—don't shoot!"

35

"Jesse?"

"Caleb!" I shouted, relieved. "Please, put the gun down."

He did, and I shone the flashlight around inside the lobby. It was just the two of us. His coat was undone, his face flushed. He pushed over a coffee table. He screamed. He smashed the butt of his rifle into the plaster walls, knocking holes everywhere. I let him rage, let him vent. He broke the glass windows of the lobby. Smashed them all out.

"Caleb . . ."

He was punching at the wall with his fist and hit a timber stud hard. He cried out in pain and slid to the ground, his back against the wall. He was out of breath, his head between his knees, and he cried. For a long time he cried. I watched him. I didn't know what to do. I felt helpless. I waited by the open doors, keeping an eye on the scene outside.

"They're gone! They're gone!" he said, over and over again. Finally there was silence as his sobbing petered out. He picked up his shotgun and walked out to the street. I followed him.

"Caleb," I said. "Mate, I'm so sorry."

Caleb didn't respond, but sniffed loudly and coughed. He aimed his gun and shot at a car, then a building, pumping out live rounds, smashing glass and metal, everything in sight. He blasted away until the gun was empty and then he stuffed a hand into his pocket and reloaded fast.

I zipped up my coat and followed him and his wrath down the street, along 71st and back towards that building that was on fire. I hoped those harmless Chasers out the front had gone. I knew I had to distract him somehow. I knew this kind of brutal loss changed you forever.

"Hey, Caleb," I said, my hand tight on his arm. "I need your help."

"How can I help you?" he screamed, pulling free. "I couldn't even help my parents!"

"Caleb—"

His eyes locked with mine and he came at me, pushing me over. "You made me do this!" he yelled. "I'd be happy to have never known what was in there, what had happened at their apartment. You made me see it all!"

I looked up at him, my friend, being pulled apart by his anger.

"You had to see it."

"Bullshit!"

"You had to, sooner or later," I said. "This is your city. You can't ignore what's happened."

"You think that's what I did?" He started pacing.

I sat up on the ground. My friend's face lit by the moon.

I said, "It's hard and it'll get harder before it gets easier."

Caleb was silent.

"What's happened is a tragedy, Caleb. I feel it too, but I can only imagine how hard it is for you. But it's what you choose to do now that counts. It's up to you, but I'd rather you didn't give up now—we need you."

He turned his back to me and paced some more. He shot at another car, just once, but it felt half-hearted. The rage had passed.

He put out a hand and helped me to my feet.

We stopped at the next intersection. I heard something far off in the distance. I watched the sky. Was it an aircraft, or just my tired ears?

"Caleb!" I said. "Listen!"

I switched off the flashlight. The two of us standing in the expanse of Park Avenue, looking south, the moon lighting the street like a runway, exposing the carnage that was spread out before us.

"Do you—"

"Shh!" he said, his head tilted to the side.

I knew he heard it too. A rumbling. Getting louder in the crisp night air.

It was cold and sad and bleak and too much. There was an explosion somewhere, several blocks south. Big. It started a chain reaction—*boom boom, boom*

boom. It went on for twenty seconds or so, no more than a second's pause between each blast. The ground shook. A car alarm went off somewhere—that was a first. It could have been anything, but nothing good.

"Come on!" Caleb yelled, and I ran after him.

We sat crouched behind a car that had crashed into the sidewalk, and watched Park Avenue, all lit up now with burning fires, some raging, some sparking, some smoldering and smoking away into the night.

"Look," he said. "A vehicle."

I knew what it was: "It's another military truck. Like the one that was attacked when I first met Felicity."

"And that's not all," he said.

"What?"

"Sounds like a drone," he said, looking from me back over the trunk of the car, the truck now three blocks out.

"A what?"

"A Predator or Reaper drone," he said, not taking his eyes off the truck that was coming our way, its lights off, driving blind. "A UAV—Unmanned Aerial Vehicle. Doesn't make sense, though."

"Why?"

Caleb looked at me. His face white and suddenly much older than mine in the moonlight.

"Because they're ours," he said.

That thought hit me hard.

"See what I mean?" he said, reading my expression. "Why would we attack our own troops like that?"

Then, before we could say anything else, the buzzing got louder. The aircraft—the drone—was coming in. It was above us in a second and flashed overhead from the north, deafeningly close, a flash of orange from under its wing and an ear-splitting explosion.

36

"**C**ome on!" he yelled, and suddenly I could hear explosions and shooting and the rumble of the truck's engine at full throttle.

We ran across Park Avenue, low to the ground, the truck now just a block away and heading towards us fast. I skidded to a stop; Caleb lost his footing on the ice and slid hard against a wall. He grabbed at his knee and stifled a scream. I rushed to help him.

"You okay?" I said, picking him up.

"Argh!" he said, hobbling next to me with his arm around my shoulder and taking cover just inside a blown-out lobby. "Knee's wrecked."

"It's bleeding," I said, seeing the blood on his hands.

"Yeah."

"Can you walk?"

"I'll be fine," he said, putting his weight on his good leg, leaning against a wall and loading his shotgun. "The soldiers were shooting out from their truck . . ."

"Yeah, but at what?" I said, peering around the stone column of the foyer, the truck finally passing us.

Visible inside the open back was Starkey, the soldier

who'd spoken to me, leaning against the big container, shooting out at—

"Down!" Caleb said.

We both saw them. Chasers, a dozen of them, running towards the truck. One was shot and fell in front of us, squirming for a moment on the icy pavement before facing us.

I gasped. "It's a woman," I said, taking a step farther back into the foyer.

"Yeah?" Caleb said, not looking away from her as she laid there, still.

"This is the first time I've seen a . . . a female Chaser, up close."

"You thought it was just men?"

"This violent kind, yeah . . . I thought maybe they were that way because they were already violent or something . . ."

Caleb pumped the shotgun's forward grip, readied to fire.

"Guess it's best not to assume anything, hey?" he said, and we stood back up cautiously, the truck slowing to nudge vehicles out of the way.

The Chasers rushed after it, but the soldiers fired back, causing three to fall. Most of the others dived opportunistically on the fresh offerings, but several held back—and then they scattered, two groups splitting away from the chase then taking cover, as though frightened.

"What are they—" I stopped. The face of one of the Chasers crouched there, bending behind a snow-covered wreck; it was that face I'd never forget, that face I saw in my dreams, that face I'd seen through binoculars from all that way up in 30 Rock. He looked away from the truck, but instead of facing us, he turned and looked up to the sky.

A buzzing, whining. I knew that sound. We all knew it.

Somewhere overhead, coming in, closing fast . . .

"Predator drone's coming in!" Caleb cried, and we ran back out to the street and away from the kill zone.

Above us, wings illuminated by the fires that ran down Park Avenue, the unmanned aircraft seemed to hone in to attack. We had only covered a quarter of a block, hugging the buildings, when the blast and shriek of the missile sounded as it tore overhead and then—

KLAPBOOM!

37

riends. Hope. I can see it all . .

F I slipped out of my thoughts and heard gunfire and screaming, felt heat, movement as if I was being dragged.

I can see my three friends, the friends I used to know, who'd stayed with me to get me through . . .

I heard a scream and could feel myself being shoved along the icy ground, forcing my eyes to blink open. In that briefest of seconds I could see a face, but then I slipped away again.

I'm in 30 Rock.

"Dave!" I yell into the empty room. "Anna! Mini!"

No answer. "Dave! Anna! Mini!" I call their names over and over.

Silence.

"Jesse! Don't move! I'll be back!" Caleb's voice loud in my ear, yelling, and it reminded me of my father, of home. A reassuring voice, it gave me hope. I began to see how my idea of home had been too simple: it was where my family was. I was beginning to think I knew where they were.

I sucked in a deep breath; intense pain, as though I was swallowing fire. I coughed and rolled onto my side to see feet shuffling past me in near darkness and the flickering orange light of fire, but no sound. Someone lay on the ground next to me, still.

Dave's joke—he never finished telling me on that subway ride. "What happens when you get those people and put them together?" That was the gist of it: four different people, what would you get? I knew now: friends for life.

I can join them now . . . But Rachel and Caleb are out there. Them and me, and Felicity, makes four. A group, a community, hope. Enough of a reason to go on. I'll figure it out. I have to. I'm a survivor.

"Caleb!" I cried, slipping back into consciousness. I could hear gunfire and screams, the crackle-bang of rounds going off in the fire-engulfed remnants of the truck. There was movement from the shadows to my left and I was knocked onto my back. I slid along the icy pavement, crashed against a car, then felt a weight on me.

A Chaser, dried blood down his front and more around his mouth, still wet, fresh, glistening from a recent feed. He was on me, pinning me down. I could see he had teeth missing. I strained to push him up and away, my hands on his chest as he clawed down at me, scratching my face, pulling my hair, desperate for more. His breath was overpowering, enough to make me retch.

I pushed up with everything I had.

BOOM!

His body went limp and he slid away.

I propped myself up on an elbow, looking at the mayhem unfolding. Caleb was there in the street, with his shotgun aimed. Caleb had saved me.

I yelled his name, but it came out hoarse and barely audible.

He dropped his shotgun, ran over to the overturned truck, still burning, and started dragging a wounded soldier away from it.

Is that Starkey? No, it's another.

Caleb slipped and got up, dragging the man faster, hobbling and struggling with his knee. To my right, three Chasers—running straight towards them.

"Caleb!" I yelled, louder this time. He looked at me.

I reached into my coat pocket for the pistol—it was not there. I looked around me, but I couldn't see it anywhere.

The soldier in Caleb's care was missing an arm. His other was wrapped around his rescuer as they headed for me, the three Chasers converging fast.

CRACK!

A Chaser fell, the gunshot from my left. I turned to look, it was Starkey. He was propped up, firing from where he sat with his back against a wall. He flicked the bolt on his rifle and aimed again.

CRACK!

Another down. The third stopped, looked at the threat, then ran off out of view.

Caleb's wounded soldier sank to the ground. I got to my feet in time to see him take his last breath.

Caleb was shaking him, telling him to get up. The two of them were backlit against the blazing inferno of what was left of the truck. Its bare frame and the fridge-sized crate were all that remained.

I ran over to Starkey. I saw he was bleeding badly, his hand bloody from where he'd been clutching at a wound to his stomach. He looked up at me, surprised, with recognition.

"What can I do?"

"Get out of here!" he tried to yell at me, his voice hoarse.

"But I can help."

"The truck!" he said. We looked across to its shell. Caleb was there, still just a few feet from it, the soldier in his arms. "We have a missile in there, in the back!"

I looked at that fridge-sized case on the bed of the truck, flames licking at it.

"A missile?"

"An unexploded missile from the attack!"

I had the image of what it would look like, as described by Caleb, crashed up against a wall in that building.

"Caleb!" I yelled. "Get over here!"

"Listen . . ." Starkey said to me, his voice weak.

I bent down to hear him. There was blood foaming on his lips.

"When it explodes," he said, "it will release the biological agent, you understand?"

"What?"

"When it gets hot enough, it will blow—it will be like the initial attack on this city."

I got it.

"You're too close, it'll get you, you'll turn into one of *them,* understand? Get away."

"Caleb!" I shouted.

"Understand?"

I nodded.

"Run!" Starkey yelled, shoving me backwards. "You can't stay here! Run!"

He picked up his rifle and I started to back farther away, away from him, from Caleb, from the truck.

I ran half a block, turned at the corner and looked at the burning street that led south, started moving again and looked back. Caleb was a black shape against the flames as he dragged another wounded man from the inferno.

"Caleb!" I yelled again. "You have to—"

KLAPBOOM!

I was blown back against a wrecked taxi, but quickly gathered my strength to get to my feet. I saw the fireball mushroom into the sky and I scrambled over the cab and ran to the next corner to catch my breath. It fogged in front of me as I watched the scene.

Where's Caleb?

I could just make out a couple of figures moving on the ground among the debris. I backed away. How far would this biological agent spread? How fast?

I kept running down the street.

Something flared up near the explosion site where the truck had been and I looked back and saw Caleb get to his feet.

"Caleb!" I yelled, but he didn't hear me, so I started back in that direction and a fire flashed bright again and I saw . . .

Caleb. At the dead body of a soldier. Drinking him.

38

This is not happening. He can't be . .
 I shook myself awake. I crossed the street, and approached my friend in disbelief.

Empty eyes stared back at me, through me. Nobody there. No recognition. Nothing. Just blood around his mouth and an unnerving fixation on me, maybe even on the blood spatters on my face. I knew for sure then that no matter what, even if it came to my own life or his, I could not kill him. Not how he was before, not how he was now. He was my friend.

Caleb.

I knew that in the aftermath, more Chasers would arrive en masse, drawn towards the scent of the newly dead. They would be on them, on whoever was left, drinking them, like sharks attracted to blood in the water.

I ran.

Why did I have to see him like that? That, as my final image of him.

I wished I had not known. Anything, anything

would have been better than what was burned into my mind's eye at that moment.

I arrived at the bookstore. The door was as I had left it. I pushed it open, fished around in the dark, tripping over several times on the mess of gear he had piled in there. I had to collect supplies if we were ever to escape this nightmare.

I slid down to the ground, sitting so I could peer out the crack of the open door to the street outside. Quiet in here, just the sound of me catching my breath in a big empty room. I looked around me, the flashlight beam searching.

I took a new backpack from its plastic cover and filled it: a few flashlights, packets of batteries, a couple of pistols and a box of live ammo, some bottled drinks and some chocolate bars. I stuffed in a few clean clothes, all too big for me; they had been stockpiled by Caleb, my friend.

Will he come back here? Will he remember this place?

I pushed those thoughts from my mind and flicked off the flashlight, looking out of the door, up and down the street. No movement, no sign of anyone, not even Chasers.

I couldn't take the bike, not in the dark, not right now. I'd come back for it, maybe tomorrow.

I flung the backpack by the door, ready to take with me, and shone the flashlight up to the top of the stairs. I pocketed Caleb's notebooks. I moved to leave, then turned back. I wrote another hope note, this time in

big block letters on the whiteboard. I only hoped he'd
be able to read it.

Five minutes later I was out on the road, the weight
of the backpack and a can of gasoline in each hand
slowing me down. I made it a block before I had to
take a break, but soon I reached the corner of Fifth
and 57th, the view north clear, the faint popping of
rifle rounds going off in the heat of the explosion just
audible.

Or maybe someone was still there, fighting.

I took a deep breath. The zoo was about seven
blocks away. I pressed on, thinking of nothing but
how the straps of my laden bag were cutting into my
shoulders, how Rachel would need this extra gas for
the generator, how loud my breathing and heartbeat
sounded. How much my head ached. How good it
would be to see Rachel and Felicity. How it would
feel to see the smiles of my friends.

I'm not afraid to be alone.

And I'm not on my own. Never have been, never will be.

39

I stopped, just for a moment. Heavy cloud cover swept in, the moon packed away for the night. I waited for a silence that would not come for my breathing and heartbeat and the sounds carried on the breeze that came from the east. An occasional gunshot. A single, dull explosion. A stifled scream.

My legs were shaking, but I had made it. The stone pillars that marked the stairs down to the arsenal building at the zoo. I collapsed to the ground, on my hands and knees, then sat there in the snow, looking up and down Fifth Avenue, at the whiteness around me. It was hours old and untouched: no one had passed through here in a while, perhaps not since I had left.

I had no energy in me. It was tempting just to rest for a bit, but my friends and their warm company were just a few more steps away. I looked down the stone stairs, slippery with ice. I stood, and slowly made my descent; legs wobbly, head throbbing, hands aching.

What will I find here?

★ ★ ★

I banged again on the front door, the broken glass rattling. I could see myself in the reflection, but I couldn't see beyond the barricade I'd built—yesterday? This morning? Was it still today?

I could hardly stand and it took everything I had to climb those few steps up to the entrance. If the girls did not hear me, I'd have to sleep out here for the night. I did not have the strength to haul myself up and over one of the tall steel fences. Here would have to do. I rested my head and closed my eyes. A moment later I jolted awake.

"Hello?" I tried to yell their names, but the sound that came out was weak and barely made its way into the building.

I sat there by the doors. I shone the flashlight around, but then switched it off, the nothingness that surrounded me melding with the night. I felt a lump under my hand, on the ground. Curious, I flicked the flashlight back on.

A little black pebble lay there next to me in the snow. It was worn smooth, almost translucent, like that volcanic glass Apache Tear I'd dreamed about. I switched off the flashlight, removed my right glove and put it in my hand. It felt warm.

Just then, I was bathed in light. Felicity appeared, shining a flashlight down to where I sat on the doorstep.

"Jesse," Felicity smiled, "hang on, I'll help you."

They helped me get warm by stoking the fire ablaze with sparking split logs wrapping my shivering body in blankets, and rubbing my back. Hot sweet cocoa coursed through me and woke me up.

I told them about the entire evening; about hiding in the plane wreck, and finding Caleb at his parents' place. And then I told them about the explosion of the recovered missile—and what it had done to my friend.

"Caleb was in the wrong place . . . he was just trying to save a wounded man," I explained. "He just wanted to do something good, you know? He just wanted to save *something*."

Felicity had been staring at me, her eyes wide, but at that she burst into tears. Huge sobs shook her small body and I moved to comfort her.

"He's— He's one of them," she said, over and over.

Rachel just sat there, silent, staring into the flames.

"It's not safe here anymore," I said, facing the fire. I turned to Rachel. "I've tried to be patient, but we have to move now, Rach. It's time we left. We need to find the other survivors at Chelsea Piers and head north. It's the only way."

Felicity was quietly nodding, backing me up, but Rachel didn't respond.

"Rachel? Don't you see? We can't stay here anymore," I said again. "The Chasers are getting smarter every day. They know how to get in here now. It's only a matter of time before they do it again. And maybe next time they'll find us—it'll be one of us dead, not just an animal."

Rachel finally met my gaze. Her eyes blazing with anger.

"Not *just* an animal?"

"You know what I mean."

"It's the Chasers and the—the whoever-the-hell are piloting those aircraft, they're the danger, they're the problem."

"We can't defend against them, Rach, you know that," I said. "Not the three of us here."

"And what about the animals, Jesse? What about *them*? You think I can just leave them here? Just walk away and leave them? You know I can't go, and I won't. This is *my* life, this is *my* choice."

"Rachel, please . . ." Felicity reached out to her, still sobbing, but Rachel stood up and pushed her away.

"No!" Rachel yelled. "Ever since you arrived, *both* of you, you've done nothing but talk about leaving. So leave already! I'm not stopping you!"

I stood. "And you'll just stay here, alone."

"I survived this long."

"You're not listening!" I said. "This isn't yesterday, or last week—it's getting worse."

"I've made my choice and I'm staying."

"Well, have you stopped to think that this is not just *your* life, Rachel?" I asked. "It's not just *your* choice. You think *I* can leave you here alone? Think we can do that? You think that's an easy thing to do? You're being selfish."

"Jesse, if Rachel—" Felicity started but Rachel cut her off.

"No, let me make this easy for you, Jesse: I don't want you here anymore. Don't need you. Everything was fine before you showed up, and now look! I was fine on my own before, and I'll be fine on my own again. Go and look for your group, go and be with your Chaser friend! I've got enough here to care about."

She stormed from the room, the door banging shut behind her.

I'd finished packing, there was nothing left to do. Felicity sat in the corner, watching. Rachel was nowhere to be seen.

"You're not coming, are you?" I said.

Felicity sighed. "You don't need me, Jesse. Rachel does."

I nodded. "Is she okay?"

"She's keeping busy, which is good," she said. "She's trying to take it in, but I think it's good, for her own sake, that she really knows what the stakes are now."

"That death's around every corner?"

"That and worse."

"Yeah," I replied. "Do you think she'll come and say good-bye?"

Felicity shook her head.

"Tell her not to worry about me."

"She will, no matter what I say."

Felicity came in close and kissed me on the cheek, pausing beside me a little longer than she had to. She was warm, her lips so soft. Outside, it was a black predawn, full of snow and wind. But when she smiled again, the day brightened.

"You know," I said, "you've got the best smile."

She beamed. "Thanks. Yours is awesome too."

★   ★   ★

This isn't home. There's a voice in my head. It's me, a part of me, but I cannot control it. It questions and reasons and rationalizes, and it remains—eternal as that southern hemisphere sunshine I imagine will be waiting for me back home. Madness? Who's to say? Maybe someone will call it that some day, some psych-something head-shrinker, some school coun- selor, maybe even my dad. Cool. Let them all analyze me and let me be there with them, wherever it is that they are, listening, talking, basking in that glow.

Felicity and Rachel need to stay on at the zoo for now, caring for the animals. I get that. I know Rachel doubts Caleb's revelation; the prospect of a whole group of survivors seems unlikely, given that the three of us remaining have only had contact with each other all these days. But I believe him, trust him; I have no reason not to. I want to meet the group at Chelsea Piers. I want to get home and the safest way for that to come about is to be with as many survivors as pos- sible. I have to find out what happened at home, just as Caleb had to—to hell with the consequences or what it might take.

I've waited too long for help that has not come. It's eighteen days since this city was attacked, and there has been no relief, no help on the horizon, no armada or airlift to offer salvation to those of us who need it. Bombs or missiles or whatever have rained down and in the hour it took me to emerge from a subway tun- nel the entire city was devastated, but that wasn't the worst of it. Eighteen days since has shown me the worst. And I know now that at least one of those who survived, uninfected by this virus, has been infected since. I cannot become like that; having survived days and weeks battling whatever's thrown at me only to become one of them.

Who knows what I might find on this trip. I'll be looking for a group of survivors and the only evidence of their existence is that my friend Caleb told me about them. Not in great detail, but he told me there was a group and that they had been talking about leaving this place. If they're there, as he said, they'll want to leave, just as he said. If they're not there, then they'll have already left. The possibility is enough for me.

I will be alone again but, hell, we do it all, everything, on our own. We enter this world alone and we leave it alone.

Meanwhile, I walk these streets full of hope. I may be the killer and the victim, but there's more to me than that. I'm a survivor.